Don't Forget Your Guidebook

DAVID WAYS

ISBN: 978-1-7397043-6-0

DEDICATED TO

Marebec

WARNING: This book contains sex, blasphemy, profanity, drugs, pain, toilets, and the views of other cultures. There's no cannibalism or threesomes, but there's plenty of satire, a giant psychedelic whale, and a ladyboy.

Contents

Contents

INTRODUCTION

TAKE OFF

"That's the most disgusting thing I've ever seen!"

"Argh, stop it already! It's not what you think."

"Your pants are covered in Vaseline," then there was that jaw twitch, followed by a sneer. "Gross … "

I said nothing. Instead, I simply scooped up my remaining clothes and moved to a different washing machine. My cure for inner thigh friction burns from running had worked. No matter what, depraved thoughts ran through Anne's head. More to the point, I had to remain calm.

My recent morning runs had shed visible layers off of my university mid-drift. She never complained about the late-night biscuit raids or tortilla fights we used to have. Not until near the end, when Anne had highlighted all this with a hefty pinch of my developing paunch. This had nothing to do with our break-up either. That was a separate issue. But all the same, I took her attempt at telling me I had put on some weight as a way that might mean I could win her back. She did like the good things in life, so I took that to mean me too.

1

Back then, such actions and comments were private. As they should be. These days, she revelled in every opportunity to take a dig at me in public. The two blokes in the laundromat looking up from their phones to see my reaction to her constant jibes could attest to that.

There was no doubting it. Anne really seemed to hate me at the moment. She spent our days together, forcing this point to fruition.

Almost as if she was trying to make me agree. Which I couldn't. Aside from giving up on our, admittedly struggling, relationship, which I wasn't, we had one last physical bond keeping us together. As a mature adult, she should put aside her petty thoughts and make the best of things.

"We're meant to be saving money." Anne ranted as she threw her jeans inside the machine. She left the door open as if to invite me back over to her side of the laundromat.

My thoughts meandered to anxiety and justification. If I didn't go over, I'd be blamed for breaking our travel budget and using two machines. If I did go over, I'd be subjected to another onslaught of verbal retribution.

"You're not putting those things in with my load either."

We were no longer mixing our underwear then.

Twenty-four hours until our flight to Bangkok and she was throwing a fit over my undergarments. Again, the whole Vaseline thing was to stop friction burns. Granted, it was messy, but it did work. I had at least four abs showing these days. In the right light. At the right angle.

What if I snuck them into the machine? She'd never know. Then I noticed the dial was pointing to 'Cool Wash'. My mum had always insisted on a sixty-degree wash. She said it killed anything living in clothes that shouldn't be there, and it got the grease out of everything.

I gave it my best shot to convince Anne.

"Are you serious? We're not going to have a chance to have a proper clothes wash for months. And, you're running a cool wash?"

The inner-nerd in me shuddered that at twenty-two I was

obsessing about laundry. It also meant a dent in masculine pride. However, this fact would redeem itself if it got on her nerves a little. A minor victory she wouldn't even know about. The lads in the corner had lost interest.

Anne's freckled jawline clenched up. Then pulsated a little. I'm not sure if it was her heartbeat that made it do that or a nervous twitch. But it meant I'd hit a nerve of some kind one way or another.

"Don't be such a Muppet, Jonny. They have laundry services in Thailand, you know?"

"Yea? So why does everybody who comes back from there look like they've not had a good wash in months then?"

"It's a fucking holiday," she spat back. "People aren't worried about their washing!"

"We're backpacking," I retorted.

"What?"

"There's a difference." There was too. "We're going for a four-month overland trip across South East Asia. Not a two-week family holiday. There's a difference."

Anne turned her palms up in exasperation. "Yeah right, that's why you spent sixty quid on bloody super wrinkle-free, smell-free shirts. You're a real backpacker, aren't you!"

"They don't need a dryer to dry," I replied in defence.

"It's 90 bloody degrees in Thailand. Everything dries!"

I stuffed one of my branded Teflon coated shirts into the machine. At least the colour wouldn't run. Not like her designer scarf a few weeks back that destroyed my last white shirt. Cranking the machine up to 60 degrees, I slammed the lid shut in defiance.

"Twat," snapped Anne. "You forgot the washing gel!" Her face went from frustration to utter disappointment.

My own jaw clenched as the machine gurgled and the door clicked tight. I fumbled with the dispenser drawer and squirted in some gel. I never knew if this was the same thing as putting it into the little cup that went inside the machine. Either way, I looked desperate. Anne stared a hole right through me with those green eyes that I once thought were so mystical.

Everyone who knew her considered me a full level under hers in terms of looks. Or, as was often pointed out, 'she's way above your league'. I didn't know which way of putting it was better for my battered confidence levels. But these levels did perk up after our first night together.

Who wouldn't want to be seen with Anne? Or more to the point actually be in a relationship with her. She was pretty much an 'it' girl in the making. The faint freckles around her eyes made her look more innocent than she actually was. Her shoulder length dark brown hair was conditioned for a maximum bounce when we went out. Back at my flat, she has always pulled it into a tight ponytail that either highlighted her determined attitude or gave her a slightly strict, but sexy, school teacher look. The latter was her career choice. Bottom line? She was gorgeous, stylish, and hot. On the negative side, she wanted to be a socialite, she did have a temper, and she didn't want us to be an official couple. Well, we can't have everything.

On the flip side, I was Mr Sensible who planned everything out, I had worked my way through Uni, and I had my own flat. Negatives? I really hadn't been outside London, I'd only had one girlfriend before Anne, and I will admit that my mum has been the most influential woman in my life, until Anne. That's why I wanted the world to know about us, but never told a soul. Maybe that's what was wrong with our relationship? We never told anyone about us. It had made things difficult.

I should have known better. I had volunteered at a student support group after seeing so many freshers struggling with 'issues' after entering the big world of tertiary education. Most of the problems were financial, exam, and relationship related. Some of the relationship stuff was rather hard going for young people to deal with. And in some cases pretty bizarre to hear how they managed to create such emotional entanglements in the first place. That said, after hearing so many stories about messed up events in people's lives, you'd think I would have learned something. Instead, we were told to listen, be supportive, help, but don't interfere and don't ask personal questions. There should have been a session for volunteers on 'don't make the same mistakes as the people you're listening too'.

Speaking of which, apparently, I was also the one that messed up our relationship. Worse yet. I was still madly in love with her. Well, maybe not madly. But I was still hoping all this was just a phase we were going through.

"What are you staring at, Jonny?" Anne's jaw was pulsating on both sides now. "Am I really going to have to put up with this for the next three months on our," she held up her fingers to mime quotation marks, "trip of a lifetime."

This will all blow over.   I was sure of it.

It had to.

Tomorrow we were flying to Thailand.

<h1 style="text-align:center">CHAPTER 1</h1>

THE ARRIVAL

Bangkok immigration looked like a giant, sterile VD clinic. Queues of humanity from all corners of the globe were all lining up up to be processed. A wonderful welcome to the land of a thousand smiles. Not that I wanted the little pudgy Thai men in their seriously too tight uniforms smiling at me for any reason other than to say move on. For the record, they didn't even say that. It was just a swift head nod to get moving along the queue.

After our 'processing', it was all quite easy. We knew where we were going. Kao San Road. An iconic road in the centre of Bangkok made famous by years of international travellers that stayed there on their way through South East Asia. It was also the only proper place in Bangkok that travellers hung out at, according to my research.

"Which way then?" asked Anne, looking around the arrivals area.

Anne, who had kept her nose in a book for most of the flight, was at least looking at me for directions now we had arrived.

I stared at the map on my phone. The words 'Connection Error' were running across the centre of the screen. Knowing where you are going is a lot easier when you're not standing in a sea of humanity, with no Wi-Fi, and two green-eyes boring holes into your soul. I had a simple way out of this.

"I think we should take a taxi …"

"What?" barked Anne. "I thought you had all this figured out. Knew the exact routes of everywhere we're staying at down to the last bus stop?" She finished with a defiant stance. "No taxis, we're on a budget, remember?"

"It's our first day here. I thought we'd take it easy." A blatant lie. My phone couldn't connect to any network to give me answers. And while the free Wi-Fi connection had a signal, there was no actual internet connection. I could only remember something about taking the train to … shwarhoburi or something.

"You're paying if we are taking a taxi."

"There's a bus," I retorted. "I remember there's a bus."

"Where?"

"To Kao San Ro…"

"I know that … where does the bus leave from?"

My backpack's left strap slipped off my shoulder and slapped to the ground, sending a small Thai lady jumping back. She scowled at me with disdain. Again, a charming welcome to Thailand.

"There's a tourist counter over there," snapped Anne, storming over to a glass cubicle covered in 'Amazing Thailand' posters.

I stood stranded on the island that was our gleaming new backpacks in the middle of Bangkok's arrivals area. All four backpacks were new and filled to maximum capacity. One contained at least one-third of Anne's wardrobe. The other contained my clothes plus Anne's makeup kit, hairdryer, and whatever else she deemed essential. Then two daypacks. Mine was at least full of my own essentials of my laptop, mobile backup that my mum had given me in case of emergencies, guidebook printouts, and allergy medicine that once again my mum had given me. Anne's daypack contained … Well, more make-up, I'm guessing. I'm not sure, really, as she wouldn't tell me. She came back just as I'd put my bags on and was wondering how her bag could only weigh twenty kilos, as it was a struggle to lift it.

"There," Anne said, pointing to a big red X on a glossy map she now possessed. "A shuttle bus leaves from here every hour. Not hard."

"Where's 'here?'" I said, reaching out for the map.

"Here!" The map was shaken at me, then pushed into her daypack.

"Where's my map?"

"Get your own."

I looked over at the tourist information desk as Anne stormed off down one of the shiny, generic corridors. I was being deserted already. All this just to get her back. I was an idiot to think this trip would work. I had to try, though. Things used to be so good between us. We were best friends. She was my first love. Well, again, there's that word. I think it was love. There was no one else before. Well, nothing serious. Anne and I had a serious relationship. Granted, it was clandestine. But all the same, we'd had a great time together, once. If that's not worth fighting for, I don't know what is.

***

They crammed the shuttle bus full of tourists, locals and various random teenagers, all staring at phones. I stared at mine. It still had no internet connection. Were they all just faking it, too? Anne was sitting at the far end, reading the glossy tourist brochure and refusing to make eye contact with me. I'd elected to stay by our bags near the main luggage rack. It was a clear demotion from chief navigator, but a lack of Wi-Fi was clearly not my fault.

We hurtled through Bangkok, I think. I couldn't see anything except for people in the bus who blocked the view. This was not good for navigation. All the same, Anne did have a window seat. Not that she seemed inclined to help. I remained calm and thought about what I'd read about the bus trip. It would leave as at the top of Kao San Road on its last stop. It couldn't go wrong. And it didn't. After forty-five minutes the bus stopped and the driver shouted out

'Kao San' twice.

The doors swung open and a mass of people both exited the bus and swarmed around the doorway outside. Various hands reached out towards the luggage rack. I gripped tightly onto our bags' straps with both hands. The straps cut into my fingers as something quite horrible washed over my body and into my lungs. Thick hot humid pungent Thai air.

With Anne finally taking her bags from me without so much as a thank you, we exited the bus.

"You wan' rooooom?"

"Come, take rooooom?"

People surrounded us. Some had no teeth. Some had glossy white teeth. Every one of them was shouting. And then there was the heat. It was unlike anything I'd ever experienced, other than a sauna. A huge mouldy, unwashed sauna heated with coals of turd and toilet water. It stuck to my skin instantly.

The myriad of locals holding up handwritten hotel signs and glossy brochures all waved frantically at us as we tried to move to the footpath. I felt like prey. They pointed at us repeatedly, then back to the brochures badly spelt highlights and blurry reproduced photographs of rooms with enormous beds. The noise was equally bewildering. A cacophony of broken English and Thai that repeated something about "Saw a Dee" or something inaudible. It was horrible and nothing like the guidebook printouts said it would be like.

Anne ploughed her way over to the doorway of a 7-11 corner store with one tout in tow. She was staring at the glossy map from the airport brochure as if I didn't exist. The store door slid open automatically and made a unique *bing-bong* sound. A waft of cool air blew out before the door slid shut and I was consumed by hot, unwashed sauna air again.

"You English, right?"

A small boy with a torn t-shirt looked up at me with a wide grin.

"I like marmalade an' toast!" he beamed in a strange Oliver Twist style of English.

"English, rrriiight?" he repeated with an all knowing grin.

"Yea," I blurted, pulling my backpack on whilst clutching at my daypack in fear of little hands going into it.

"London? Birrrrminghammm? Issssliiingon?"

"No, Oxford?" I said, looking past the boy. There was an old Thai lady behind him staring holes into my head by the side of the road. She didn't look happy to see us behind her table of what looked like lottery tickets.

The 7-11 door slid open again. *Bing Bong*. The cool air was an instant relief for all of 4 seconds before the door slid shut again.

"Rowing, you like to row, mate? Beat Cambridge again, did you, mate?"

"How … what?" I couldn't quite comprehend how the small Thai boy could (a) speak with a cockney accent and still mispronounce things. (b) knew about Oxford rowing. (c) why he was telling me all this.

"Jonny??"

It was Anne. She was glaring over at me from beside the old lady's table. I moved closer to her, only to get a look of death from the old lady.

"CHAW CHAW MY HINNI!" squawked the old lady as she pointed angrily at me. Was she cursing me? I'd only just arrived.

Bing-Bong went the door.

I moved away from the old lady's pointing finger and stood over a metal grill on the footpath. Impossibly, it was bellowing out a constant stream of hot air. Only this heat had the sickly odor of moist sewer. Was the entire city like this? One giant bellow of fetid heat!

Bing-Bong.

A customer entered the 7-11. I was now too far away to feel the blast of cold air. The old lady started shouting about me to another old lady further down the road. The sewer heat smell changed to something rancid as it thundered up from the metal grill beneath me. None of this was in the guidebook. None of it.

"Missssta, I help," the young boy began tugging at my daypack.

"No!" I grabbed it back. "It's got my laptop in there."

I honestly regretted blurting that out. I took a mental note never to do it again.

"Yea sure," nodded the boy. "You want a room with Wi-Fi and double bed with you girlfriend."

"Jonny, come on!" scowled Anne as she stomped across the footpath.

Shaking my head at the boy, I hugged my bags tighter and followed Anne across the road past a throng of Australians in tank tops. It was a bizarre sight. They were all wearing an assortment of wild afro style wigs whilst most carried small cans of beer in each hand. Where the hell was I?

Kao San Road. The most popular backpacker hang-out in all of South East Asia. Well, at least one road was Kao San. There were several roads at the intersection where we were crossing, but I couldn't quite see any street signs pointing to the actual Kao San Road. Again, none of this was in the guidebook. All I knew was that I was now feeling decidedly ill from the hideous smells engulfing me and the amount of sweat I was producing just from a short walk.

"Jonny," glared Anne once we'd crossed over. "Do you know where this Cherry Inn is exactly, or not?"

I dropped my day pack onto my feet. "I need a drink."

"For fuck's sake Jonny, let's get to the hostel first!"

"It's off Soi 11 … I think," from what I remember from the online booking form, anyway. Not that they had any street signs in Bangkok to make it easier.

"Cherry's bad matey, no Wi-Fi?"

Anne stared down at the small boy who'd followed us over. Then she looked up at me and shook her head disapprovingly.

"It's okay," she said, looking at the boy with one of her forced smiles. Beads of humid, enforced sweat formed on her brow. "We've a reservation there."

The boy turned his smile upside down in a theatrical gesture. "No good, no Wi-Fi. An' is a full one hour ago. Lots walk-in customer."

"What? It's full?" I blurted.

"Yea, I show you Sao La Lodge. Good price."

I looked at Anne. She looked back at me with less contempt and with a hint of confusion.

"Young man," she said with a stern, but kind smile. "Are you quite sure?"

The boy put his hands on his hips and pushed out his cheeks with air. Anne laughed, and the boy broke out into a big smile.

"You are a nice lady," he said matter-of-factly.

"Why thank you," replied Anne. "It's nice to have a proper gentleman around here who knows his way around."

"It's a good place," beamed the boy. "Honest."

Bing-Bong.

The 7-11 across the road never shut up. Why was the noise even necessary? Did the staff really need a noise to know when someone walked in? Or just walked by outside close enough to set the sensor off? Could they not adjust it slightly?

The old lady was no longer glaring at me. My shirt had now changed from light green to dark green. I physically felt like the remaining liquid inside me had evaporated. Strangely, sweating made no difference to how hot I felt. In fact, it made me feel worse. Everything I wore was now sticking to me and making me feel like a hot, soggy toilet roll. How could people live like this? This was not normal. Not normal at all. None of this was in the guidebook photocopies. We needed to get out of here, fast.

"No harm in looking at his place?" I suggested in desperation.

"Not far," the boy started again. "Just around corner, good Wi-Fi. Very clean. Very Niiccce. Commmeeee on."

"We can just take a look?" I urged. "Surely they had to have air-conditioning? We could just sit in reception and plan out what to do."

Anne shrugged. That meant yes.

Maybe, just maybe, if I could get this right, all would be well with the world again. And maybe Anne would forgive me.

CHAPTER 2

PAST AND PRESENT

"I'll never listen to you again … EVER!"

The small boy had stitched us up… Still, I don't know why Anne was complaining so much. It's not as though we were staying in an utter dump. It's just that the original place we booked was nicer. All the same, Anne insisted, we went to the original guesthouse we had booked. It was only two streets away. As it turned out, they were not booked out like the boy had said. Unfortunately, according to the receptionist, we could not get a refund because we never checked in. Or more to the point, we would not get a refund as we'd checked in somewhere else.

Anne sat on what would have been our guesthouse's doorstep. Hands on cheeks, she looked out into the quiet side street. I sat down beside her, hoping to show some sort of mutual respect for getting done over by a boy of at least ten. She purposely shuffled over to the far edge. There seemed to be no way to win her back. So much had changed between us so quickly. So much so that I was still having a hard time piecing it all together.

In my final year of University I joined a study group with Charles, one of my best mates, and Anne's big brother. We desperately needed pre-written papers for our finals. The group also had a great discount club for just about anything a student could want.

Ten percent discounts to the Icon cinema on Wednesdays. Free up sizes at a popular deli. Friday night half price drinks at Elliot's. And, an end of Uni interest free 'Freedom Flight' promotion. It was a great idea. Put in a monthly cash subscription towards a select destination at the end of the school year. If you saved enough, you could get a substantial discount on a return flight to India, Thailand, Greece or some crime ridden beach in Mexico. We signed up, but Charles had been offered an internship at some solicitors firm so he offered the subscription to Anne. For me, it meant an easy way to save and something to look forward to as I still hadn't a clue what to do with an arts degree.

It was during all this I met Anne, properly. I'd met her a few times at Charles' house growing up. She was one of those dreary nose-in-the-book types of younger sisters. Half braless hippie, half bookworm.

That all changed last summer when Anne burst out of her hippy world and lay glistening in golden tanning lotion on Charles' back lawn. She had dumped the hippie ways and become a 'socialite'. That's also when I got my first warning from Charles.

"Touch it, and you're dead."

I gave a shocked dismissive look and then pealed myself away from the window overlooking the back garden.

"I know what type of post-pubescent wanker you are," he continued. "Both mentally, and between your sheets at night."

"Piss off Charles, it's bloody Anne. Ms. Harry bleedin' Potter lovin' Anne."

He gave me one of those looks and that was the last we spoke about it. A Cuban theme night at Elliot's with mojitos on tap would help me forget his warnings. Wrapped up in a blur of minted rum, I remember stalking Anne from afar while wearing a rainbow coloured poncho. I didn't have a clue if Cubans wore ponchos, but it was all I could muster up.

Anne didn't get the Cuban vibe either. It didn't matter. She was wearing one of those straw Panama hats. A neon pink half-cut t-shirt. Boot cut jeans with big black cowgirl boots to match. This was no longer Hogwarts. I was like a lamb to the slaughter.

There's something about the untouchable and unobtainable that appealed to me. That and the raw power of fresh-smelling mint fuelled alcohol at two a.m. Anne seemed to be on the same wavelength. Though I did briefly wonder if she had the ulterior motive of rebelling against her overprotective brother. There was once a time he beat the hell out of a guy who dumped her for another girl at the last minute before her secondary school graduation bash. As for me, all I remember was a brief discussion on how easy it was to remove a poncho compared to a neo pink t-shirt. And the sheer feeling of sobering panic the next morning.

"He can never find out ..."

I remember the pain in my eyes like they'd been used as nails by mint crushing hammers. Anne was lying next to me. Her arms stretched upwards and crossed succinctly above her head as if handcuffed. The panic left instantly in a sea of surging testosterone.

"Get off!"

My head returned to its pounding with reckless abandon as Anne pushed me back. Did I still smell of rum? Perhaps she was suffering, too.

Take it easy, Jonny.

Slow down.

I was in that semi-drunk next morning dream-like haze. Nothing really sunk in.

"Gawd ... what was I thinking?" she sat up pulling the bedsheet with her.

"Relax," I cooed. Both to Anne and myself. "It's my apartment. We're fine here."

Anne wrinkled her nose and I could see the tension ease from her shoulders.

"How?" she started, but then rephrased her question. "How'd you afford your own place, anyway?"

I don't know what triggered my mind, but I knew this was an important question. Or more to the point, the answer was important. I went with the quasi-truth.

"Well, my parents," I began, but then noticed a small frown on Anne's face appearing. I needed to be more independent.

"My parents," I started again. If she could, so could I. "They gave me a choice. A car, apartment deposit, or lump sum. That was the deal for going to a university away from home."

"Oh, so you own it!"

"No," I laughed. "I'm renting. But the deposit was good enough to get my own place rather than sharing."

"Really?"

"Yep, all mine. They thought it would help me to study better and all that."

"It is handy, I suppose."

"What do you mean?"

"To have your own place while at Uni," replied Anne with a little bit of a congratulatory nod. "I mean, not many people have their 'own' place at university."

She was right. I knew it. My parents knew it. We all knew it. All the same, I did have to work to pay the rent, too. But that didn't seem like the right thing to say here. It seemed I impressed Anne by having my own place. In hindsight, it was a mistake to capitalise on this. But my hormones told me otherwise.

"Yea, I can have all the privacy I want." I smiled. "Invite who I want over whenever I want and all that."

"So you can," said Anne, hiding a slight smile. "I always wanted you Anne," my hormones were taking over again. "Always. You're amazingly beautiful. So perfect."

Her face changed. That small hidden smile turned into a lip-bitten smile. She lifted up the single sheet and rolled over onto me.

"You're so wicked Jonny ..."

And that was that. If Charles ever found out, I'd be pulverised.

Our friendship would be ruined. My parents would never help me out like this again. And I'd be blamed for 'corrupting' Anne. We both knew this wasn't the case. Yet, somehow, we both found it a turn on. The Charles finding out part, not the pulverising part. The corrupting Anne thing too. Well, at least in my case. Even if it was a fantasy. In truth, it was probably the other way around.

***

It was hard to believe we spent an entire summer making secret rendezvous and avoided all eye contact when around Charles. If only he saw what she was like today. On second thoughts, having Charles see any of this would not be good for my health.

"Maybe a drink?" I suggested.

Anything to break the silence and the fact we were sitting in, at least, 50 degrees worth of heat with an added 200% of suffocating Thai humidity.

Nothing. Not even a shuffle or jaw clench.

I stared out at the little quiet street. Streams of tatty black cables ran along the mishmash of corrugated tin-roofed buildings. Nothing was uniform here. Even the unpainted concrete walls were different shades of grey. The terraced houses all looked so random. Some had odd extensions, walls, gates, railings, and roofing added on at a whim's notice. And, by the looks of it, built by a person with no idea what structural integrity meant.

The Thais themselves were an odd bunch. Sometimes full of smiles. Usually, a smile only occurred when you were handing over a wad of cash to them. Otherwise, they were scowling at you from a distance. The smilers were often dressed in nice fresh looking clothes. The scowlers in saggy clothes that looked like Oxfam handouts.

I noted Thai men seemed to have problems growing beards. I'd never noticed this before in my entire life. Or at least once in people over the age of eighteen. In fact, come to think of it, Thai men didn't even have light stubble. A hairline moustache was quite common. The type you'd see on a third former back home. What the Thais had, that nobody else had, were a few people with very long wiry hair growing from a mole or the end of a chin. Gender didn't seem to matter in this case either. The older the Thai, the more chance the man or woman would sport at least one wiry foot long hair on their face. It wasn't flattering either. It made me feel obsessive compulsive and want to yank the hairs out and go 'there, that's better now, isn't it?'

Thais didn't seem to like tourists around here either. We were definitely cash cows to them. Unless you were handing them money, they wanted nothing to do with you. So much for Asian friendliness. I was here half a day already and just knew it wasn't for me. It would have been better if I'd booked the Greek flight. But no, Anne liked the idea of a trip to Asia. Europe just seemed more fun, safe and easy. We would have been nearer to home too. The thought of my mum's home cooked dinner suddenly pulled across my stomach. Jet lag meant we'd missed out on a dinner or was it a breakfast?

"Maybe some food?" I suggested. "We've not eaten properly since yesterday. Let's say we try out some of this Thai food everyone rants on about?"

Anne didn't budge.

"My treat."

Nothing.

"We can come back here tomorrow?" I said, getting just a little fed up with the pouting.

She turned to me, looking quite exacerbated.

"I'm going back for a shower. I'll eat later."

"But I'm hungry."

"Then go eat! I'm going back."

"How will we meet up later?"

Anne didn't answer. And for the second time, she walked away from me in Bangkok without even a hint of responsibility. We were meant to stick together when travelling abroad. It was written in big bold writing on all guidebooks. It was dangerous to travel solo in places like Thailand. Anything could happen. Charles would beat me to death if anything ever happened to her. It was his golden rule 'no harm shall come to Anne.' I'd broken it by sleeping with her. Trampled on it by dating here. Yet all the same, this was different. We were no longer in Blighty. Of all places and scenarios, we should be looking out for each other here. Hence, she was doing this.

Watching Anne walk away, I thought about calling out once more. Then, just as I was about to swallow my pride, I realized I had no clue how to get back to our new guesthouse. Heck, I couldn't even pronounce the name of it properly. I had to follow her like a stalker. If questioned, I would say I didn't want her to walk home alone. That was an appropriate answer that solved two problems. Yet it didn't solve my hunger problem. Nor how this holiday was ending up.

CHAPTER 3

ENTER THE DRAGON

It seemed most of Bangkok's free Wi-Fi had a signal. But, no actual internet connection. It was a similar situation at our new guesthouse. Leaving Anne to shower, I gobbled up some oat bars I'd stashed in my bag and took my first walk down Kao San Road by myself in search of an actual working internet connection to call my parents. I also needed to let Charles know everything was going fantastically well with our trip. Yes, it was all lies, but nobody wanted to know anything else.

In truth, as you may have guessed, Bangkok has not impressed me so far at all. There was a distinct lack of temples, praying monks, and serenity. It all seemed to be replaced by outdoor bars that wouldn't feel out of place along a London bar district. 7-11 stores. And drunk tourists. Why do guidebooks put photos of temples and beaches all over their books when the first thing you see are drunken tourists at a bar? They weren't typical tourists either. They were like a cross between drunk soccer fans on a stag night at some street party in Soho. The not so expensive part of Soho, if that still exists.

On the quieter side of things, overweight tattooed white men in soccer shirts lounged with iced beer while skinny, pretty local girls sat beside them. In some cases, not so pretty, but still very skinny. I'll redo my Soho example. They were like drunken soccer louts taking part in a bar scene from Apocalypse Now. Yes, that was a closer match.

The obsessive humidity gave it all a distinctive tropical feel, but without the palm trees. In fact, there didn't seem to be any trees or vegetation around. Also, unlike in London, I couldn't walk past a bar without at least three Thais coming up to me with multiple brochures in hand. Each one offering much the same thing.

"Massssage sir?" asked a girl in a tight red dress.

"No, thanks."

"You wan Massssage ..." asked another, wearing far too much make-up for this heat.

"No thanks, I'm good."

"Free drinnnnk sir, you want to come??" beckoned a rather attractive Thai girl who somehow came across like she wanted to devour me with her eyes alone.

"Maybe later," I smiled back.

She looked me up and down, then dismissed me with a raise of her eyebrow before turning away on her heels. My mind wandered for a second before a strange underweight Thai man waved at me like he was my long-lost best friend.

"What you need, friend?"

"Just looking for internet".

"Yes sirrrr, free WiFyyyy."

I stopped and looked at the underweight man in his forties as he tried to hand me a drinks menu. "You have Wi-Fi?"

"Yes sir," he said, smiling to reveal a solitary front tooth along with the remanents of yellowing stubs of teeth. "We have WiFyyyy. Free with the beer too. Come sit."

Guided by my Wi-Fi promising toothless long-lost friend, we entered his neon lit beer garden. Again, despite being a tropical country, the potted plants around the outside of the bar looked decidedly plastic. The man took the lead; it was only now I noticed he was swinging his hips like only a super model could. It was odd, and I wasn't sure if he was a few shots short of a tequila bottle or just unexpectedly effeminate. We stopped by a table that overlooked the road. As I sat down, he waved his hand up and down as if showcasing a new car. Flamboyant wasn't the word. I cringed into my seat, hoping nobody thought I really was his long-lost friend.

"It's a kinda hot out here," I said, trying not to make eye contact with the nearby table of beer swilling Australians. Their loud conversation revolved around some local girls this morning, their body parts, and their body parts ability. The type of background conversation my mother should not be subjected to.

"Inside sir, air-con," replied my ever effeminate server.

The moment we walked inside, the mood changed. The lighting got dimmer, and the air became instantly cooler. My brain relaxed with the feeling of normal cold air rushing up to me. The customers seated over cramped tables looked a little different, too.

Beer glasses were replaced with white coffee cups, while laptops and iPads replaced the skinny girls for companionship. More importantly, the Wi-Fi worked and was strong enough to call mum to let her know I'd arrived safely. And lie by saying repeatedly that I was really enjoying Thailand.

Then there was the call to Charles. Another person who'd sworn me to keep regular updates for fear of a death threat should anything happen to his sister, Anne. Thankfully, he wasn't around, so I left a voice on FB messenger.

"Charles mate. Just arrived. The place is bloody awesome. Wild. Massive stuff going on. We checked into a really great little guesthouse. No Wi-Fi, but free breakfast. Anne's there now, chilling out with some awesome people we met. Anyway gotta go, am at a bar and there's some really hot chicks around here! Cheers, catch you later."

I looked up and noticed the stare. A raised eyebrow of dubious suspicion from a guy sitting at a table opposite mine. The stranger then looked my effeminate server up and down as he, or possibly a once upon a time she, stood beside me with a class of beer. I could see his point about staring. A single toothed man in his forties with the stance of a twenty-year-old supermodel.

"You wan' pay now, or laterrr?"

I was still enjoying the cold air. So my host kept offering alternative ways to pay.

"Cash? Creeedit card? I run a tab?"

"Tab, like I can pay later?" I repeated to a blank stare.

"No problem, I make you own bill."

"Like a tab, you mean?" I repeated.

"I probably wouldn't do that if I were you."

It was the guy from the other table.

"Come again?"

"The tab," he said, pointing with a nod towards the server. "It has a tendency to increase the price."

I stared at the stranger sitting behind a big black laptop screen, unsure why he was butting in like this. Maybe it was the thing to do in a place like Thailand. Stick up for other tourists. I figured it couldn't do any harm either way, so I paid upfront for the beer. My host took the five hundred baht note I offered and skulked off with a lesser swing of the hips.

"Thanks mate." I said, acknowledging the man by raising up my glass of beer.

The laptop stranger nodded again, barely looking up from his screen. A big guy with dark spiky hair, he seemed a little out of place here. Wearing well worn cut off combat shorts and a multi-pocket North Face shirt, he looked more akin to a jungle trekking guide than a backpacker out for a good time.

"You might need to chase after your change too," he said, not looking up from his laptop.

I couldn't place his accent. Canadian, Australian or a mix. He reached over to a large mug of coffee and drank from it. Then noticed me staring at him.

"Uhhh thanks again mate," I said in defence of my stare. "Just arrived. Still trying to get a feel for the place."

"No problems," he said, nodding slightly as if he was used to it.

"No changeeeeee." My host was back holding my five hundred baht note like a wet fish.

"What'd you mean, no change? It's a bar, isn't it?"

"No changeeee."

"Well, neither do I!"

My host, for only the second time, let loose a wide single toothed grin, "I keep change?"

"No!" I blurted out, "That's a lot of money ... I think. Why don't you have change?"

"I've two hundred," said the laptop guy, reaching over with a couple of Thai notes. "You can pay for my coffee and your beer with your five hundred and keep my two hundred. It'll save you some hassle"

My host didn't wait for a reply. He disappeared off with a waddle and my five hundred baht note.

"Uhhh, thanks." I wasn't sure what quite happened. Jet lag must have been kicking in. But everything had returned to normal. So, it must have been good.

"Don't worry about it," said the laptop guy, half standing up and extending his hand. "This shit happens all over this place. The name's Stuart by the way."

"Oh, Jonny," I replied, shaking his clammy hand. "Thanks again. You mean this shit happens in this bar or Bangkok."

Stuart sat back down. Wiped his hand on his shorts and shrugged, "Probably Thailand." He paused before shaking his head in disagreement with himself. "Naw, not all of Thailand. Just the touristy places. They'll take you for everything you're worth."

"Really?"

"Sorry," Stuart continued with a frown. "Thailand's not my favourite of places, so take everything I say with a grain of salt. But it's not a bad assumption to say most people are out for what they can make in Bangkok. Kao San Road in particular. It's certainly much better in remoter areas. Good people out there, like in most places."

I nodded in mild, thoughtful agreement at the barrage of information. The most I picked up on was that he didn't like Thailand either!

"Don't let me put you off, though. Enjoy it for what it's worth."

Finally, it looks like I wasn't the only person to think Thailand wasn't the best of places. Granted, we'd only just arrived. But from the bars, bar girls, and bar customers, it seemed the whole place was anything but 'Amazing Thailand'.

"Can you recommend any place to go without all the hassles?" I said in the meek hope of getting some knowledge to impress Anne with.

Stuart shrugged in mild irritation and then proceeded to let me in on some of his preferred places in Thailand. Apparently, up north was where the culture was and down south was where the beaches were. Bangkok was, well, Bangkok.

I thought about how badly I had researched our trip. How I thought photocopies of guidebook chapter highlights would do instead of the real thing. We'd never get off the beaten path with what I'd copied. How I thought we'd just arrive and join in with some other backpackers from our guesthouse. Unfortunately, our new guesthouse had no common room. And the only signs of life seemed to come from the long bathroom queues. Yes, to Anne's chagrin, our guesthouse didn't have a private bathroom. And yes, the first one did.

"Can I ask you another question?"

Stuart looked up at me briefly and shrugged.

"What's with the long wiry hair coming out of some people's faces here? It's a bit off, isn't it?"

Stuart's face scrunched up. It was an awkward question. But it had been bothering me since we arrived.

"I think," answered Stuart. "It's to do with luck. The longer the hair, the more luck it brings."

"Oh," I replied. "That's different".

"So is not walking under a ladder or sweating non-stop."

"Huh?"

"Well," explained Stuart, looking around my face. "You're a bit shiny there. And you have sweaty patches under your arms. To Thais, that's pretty gross."

"It's hot," I said in all honesty.

"It sure is," replied Stuart rather bluntly. "But it's normal for Thais. It's not normal for you. The same with the long little fingernail. That's also a luck thing here."

"I haven't noticed that."

"You will." Stuart smiled before looking back at his laptop.

He was right. I didn't have a clue about Thai culture other than some Thai dishes. I was the visitor here. I remembered flicking over the 'Learn About Thailand' section of some websites I had browsed when looking for the best places to eat in Bangkok. That was about the sum of my Thai cultural understanding.

Then, as I stared out the window wondering why I was here, I saw Anne walking by outside. Burdening Stuart yet again, I quickly asked him to mind my beer as I ran out to wave down Anne. She wasn't impressed I'd spotted her.

"Stuart, Anne,"

I introduced them as best I could, considering neither of them seemed that happy at being disturbed. "Stuart's been here a while. I think."

"Really?" asked Anne. My first victory. The first backpacker friend we'd come across was mine to find, not hers.

"I think this is my ninth time here." Stuart replied as if it was a round of golf he was talking about.

"What, really?" clamoured Anne. "You like it that much?"

"No, just passing through."

"Oh," I said, trying to tie things up a little. "You're heading somewhere else on holiday?"

Stuart shook his head with a strange wry smile. Then looked up and gave his answer to Anne, and not to me. "No, I'm working. Just passing through. I'm a travel writer."

"A travel writer!" gasped Anne.

Stuart shrugged as if it meant nothing.

"How incredible! Do you like work for a guidebook or a magazine or what?"

Shit. I'd lost control within milliseconds. He wasn't on holiday. He wrote about the bloody things. And Anne was hooked on him instantly.

"No, I'm freelance," replied Stuart.

Anne gasped again. I wish she'd calm down a bit. I couldn't see any actual excitement in all this. Freelance meant unemployed. Though in Anne's eyes, it probably meant a rebel with a cause.

"I mix it with travel photography to make ends meet."

"A photographer too!" Anne threw her hands up and exhaled rather too loudly. This was getting embarrassing. I was beginning to dislike Stuart.

"Can I join you?" asked Anne.

What? Where was she joining him? Things were getting out of hand. Neither of them were even acknowledging me.

Stuart nodded with a calm shrug. Anne sat down at his table without so much as a glance towards me. Stuart lowered his laptop screen and smiled at Anne.

I really didn't like Stuart.

CHAPTER 4

THE KNOW IT ALL AND THE ESCAPE PLAN

After using the excuse that I had to research our trip a little more, I finally relented and moved to Stuart's table. It had nothing to do with the fact I had been sitting there and was being completely ignored. However, my move seemed rather pointless as both Stuart and Anne were so deeply entrenched in conversation they didn't even notice. Anne was in full swing with her questions.

"So we have to wear long pants and shirts to visit the royal palace?"

"Yea," Stuart nodded as if he was a walking Lonely Planet. "Otherwise they won't let you in. Oh, and make sure to buy your tickets at the gate and not outside."

"Why?" Anne asked, as if her life depended on it.

"Touts. Bangkok's full of touts. They'll tell you anything to make a sale and sell you anything even if it doesn't exist."

Anne then pieced together our arrival and the boy telling us our guesthouse was full. Most of this revolved around me being the one at fault.

Stuart nodded, as if everything was obvious. "Yep. That sounds like Bangkok. Everywhere is full when you arrive. At least according to the touts waiting for you outside your bus. You should see the scuffles if they say it in front of another tout from an empty hotel!"

Anne let loose a hideous high-pitched laugh and slapped her hand on the table. She was falling for all this?

"You gotta watch out for the watered down beer too," for the first time since sitting down Stuart looked over at me. Or rather, my glass of beer. "Better you buy bottled beer. It costs a little more, but it won't be watered down."

"You're only telling me this now?" I chirped in. Feeling duped by Stuart paying for my beer earlier.

"You'd already bought the beer," he replied, looking mildly shocked. He then smiled as if the world was his oyster. "And I think I helped you pay for that beer too?"

"Yea but …"

"So no beer in glasses," interrupted Anne. "No shorts at the palace, and no …"

"No being led to hotels by touts."

Anne shot me a look. Sighed. Then went into her handbag to pull out a notebook. "I'm going to start writing all this down. Do you mind?"

Mother of gawd. This was getting pathetic. Why didn't she just come out and ask him to be our tour guide. Or better yet, invite him out for dinner so she can spend the next two hours drooling over Mr Lonely Planet.

"It's fine," shrugged Stuart as if he was asked this every day. "But really, if you just buy a guidebook it's all in there, anyway."

"That was his job." I got a second glance from Anne. "So we don't have any, of course. Just some photocopies."

"I saw some for sale outside," I replied, as if it had been my plan all along.

"Just be sure to look inside the cover first."

"Why?" I said, looking back in irritation.

"Because most of the guidebooks they sell out there are fakes."

"Really?" gasped Anne, taking another note.

"Yea, photocopies. Some have the latest colour covers, but inside you can read the publishers' page and see it dates back a few years. And the maps are no good."

"Out of date too?"

"Well, everything is. But the maps rarely copy well. They are so faded you can't read them."

"We'll buy from a bookstore then," I quipped.

"Go to the Paragon store. It's just off the BTS."

Was there anything this guy didn't know? If I asked him how much the book cost, I'd guess he'd know down to the nearest penny. I didn't dare ask what the BTS was.

Anne was already having Stuart mark out the location of the Paragon store on her glossy map. Then quickly they moved on to must see sights in Bangkok. I noticed her hands touching his as he swung a pencil over the map all knowingly, in wide arcs. Apparently, the BTS was Bangkok's city rail service. Why he couldn't say railway or train? I don't know.

"So where are you from, anyway? I asked.

"A little bit of everywhere," replied Stuart, not looking up.

"Ha, where's that then?"

No answer.

"I can't place your accent?"

"Been travelling a long time. My accents also from a little bit of everywhere," he ended with a chuckle and gave a wide smile to Anne. I could swear I heard her coo in reply.

"You've got to be from somewhere?" I retorted.

"Jesus, Jonny, will you stop already!" snapped Anne. "Can't you tell Stuart's been travelling the world a long time. He's been to many places and I'm sure he's got to know many cultures. He's a true global citizen."

I nearly retched.

"When that happens, you really do become a part of everywhere."

she continued.

"Aw come on ..."

"That's pretty much a nail on the head," Stuart said with another smile to Anne.

Then a miracle occurred. Stuart looked at his watch and announced he had to go. Anne was visibly gutted. I think my heart rate increased in anticipation.

He apologised while closing up his laptop and packing it away. I shook my head in commiseration. It was getting dark and apparently he was only in Kao San Road to take some night-time photos of the street.

"Can we join you?" asked Anne.

I winced. How desperate can one person sound?

Again, another sweet mercy saved us. Stuart shook his head and explained it was all rather boring. Lots of standing around waiting for moments to photograph. Very boring stuff indeed. He was actually shaking us off. Quite well, too, I thought. Maybe he wasn't so bad after all.

Trying to save face, Anne mentioned something about not having eaten yet. Stuart, naturally enough, made a suggestion of where to get the best local food without being ripped off. Then he handed Anne a business card. He eventually handed me one, too.

"That's my website if you want to take a look," Stuart said, picking up his bag. "Oh, and my email address is on there too if you ever want to say hello."

Anne looked up at him as if he'd just thrown her a life jacket. I typed his website into my phone. Damned if the first thing that didn't hit me was a huge photo of Mount Everest. I turned my phone away from Anne's line of vision.

"How come there's no Lonely Planet writer on here?" I asked, breaking up their goodbye handshake.

"Sorry?"

"You said you were a travel writer. Haven't you worked for them?"

"No," he grinned tightly. "I don't think I would want to either. They automate most of their guidebook writing these days."

"So who have you done work for?" I clicked on his about page and drew my face closer to the screen.

"I'm freelance."

"So nobody?"

Anne shot me an evil look.

"No," Stuart replied slowly. "I do work for various people who are looking for articles on things. Magazines, websites …"

"You mean you just write for blogs," I said, clicking on his own blog.

Stuart frowned and looked frustrated.

"I've done work for travel websites and blogs."

"So you're just a travel blogger then?"

"I'm not a travel blogger!"

Bingo. Stuart was now officially pissed off.

"So why does it say blog on your website?"

"Because there's a blog on it," he gasped. "Have a look around. You'll see it's different from most websites."

"Nah," I pushed my phone into my pocket. "I don't really like blogs that much."

"Liar," butted in Anne. "You're always reading online."

"Yea, but …"

"I'm sorry about Jonny," continued Anne. "He's just being a pain these days."

Stuart shrugged it all off as if it meant nothing. But I knew that I'd just got under his skin. Shame Anne couldn't see it too.

"Will you be staying around Bangkok?"

"No, I'm leaving tomorrow."

Anne's shoulders dropped. And I suddenly felt a lot better.

"Tomorrow?"

"Yea, I'm taking the train north to Chiang Mai."

"Chiang Mai?"

"Yea, it's cooler up there and I want to stay awhile to work on my book."

"Book?"

Fuck.

"You're writing a book?!"

Anne's excitement was getting embarrassing. And Stuart took it all like it meant nothing to him. She put on a little sad smile as Stuart gave her a little wave goodbye.

I grinned from ear to ear. Thank god that was all over with.

CHAPTER 5

TOURING THE LAND OF THE BUDDHA

Our first full day in Bangkok was going to be our day of culture, exploring the unknown and true independent travel. Anne was keen to see some of Thailand's temples and while not overly excited at that prospect, I was happy not to be the brunt of her vexed anger this morning.

We avoided the touts, starting with our receptionist trying to get us on a local temple tour with other guests. Then it was on to the road outside our guest house, which was now a row of tuk tuk drivers, all flapping lamented Bangkok maps at us. Kao San Road was strangely quiet aside from some early morning calls for 'massaaages'. Even the oppressive heat seemed to be slightly less insufferable in the morning. I say that as only the back of my shirt was sopping wet after 5 minutes of walking.

Via my photocopied map, we made it to one of the small ferry stops that line Bangkok's main river. After the small hic-up of trying to figure out what boat would take us directly to the Grand Palace, we ended up with tickets to take us on a half-day river tour. No one would give us a straight answer about direct boats. In fact, anytime we tried to ask for anything, the answer was nearly always 'Yes'.

That's a yes with a smile. Normally followed by an extended hand looking for money.

"Can we get a boat ticket to the Grand Palace?"

"Yes, you buy tour here."

"No, just a boat ticket to the Palace directly."

"Yes, buy here."

"No, that's a tour office. We just want a boat."

"Yes, buy boat ticket."

"Yes, buy boat ticket without tour."

"No."

"Yes."

We bought the tour ticket.

The good news was I made Anne laugh for the first time when I asked the girl giving out tickets if they included "complementary massaaaages." Yes, finally things were looking up this morning.

A loud engine powered our long-boat that bounced above the wide river's choppy waves. Nobody wore life jackets. I'm not sure we even knew where they were. It didn't matter; the boat felt safe and the warm wind felt cooler than it did standing around at the dock. Anne was smiling alongside me. I let her enjoy the moment.

We pulled up outside another dock after about ten minutes and were bundled out. Nobody told us where to go or when we should come back. We ignored the fact that we had bought a 'tour' because everyone else ignored this fact too. Everybody just went with the flow, so we followed some people outside and across the road to the gigantic walls that surrounded Thailand's Royal Family's equivalent to Buckingham Palace. The Grand Palace. It seemed Dante had arrived before us, as it was getting hotter with every passing minute.

"Glad you wore your long pants, aren't you?" chirped Anne.

All I could think of was, no. They were making me hotter. So hot that after sitting on the boat for just 10 minutes, I felt sure I had a soggy bottom from sweat. It was gross, but that's Thailand for you. However, I knew what she meant, so stayed quiet. This was proving difficult, though.

We stood looking at multiple signs with multiple rows of rules and regulations in various languages on what they required to enter the Grand Place. Stuart had been correct about the dress code. Anne was reminding me. Rather than setting her off, I just raised my eyebrows and patted my damp pants.

"You wannnn guide sir?"

Thais had tourism tied up. You couldn't turn left without some smiling person standing in front of you flashing some faded 'tour guide' ID or laminated map in your face. We shook our heads and ducked under a few more before buying the tickets from the official counter. We opted to use my photocopies and a map Anne had found at the guest house to show us around.

"You wannnn ice cream sir?"

Another tout. This time, a micro-sized girl in an oversized basketball shirt that swamped her little frame. We'd not even made it past the tour guides when the next line of touts offering food and drink descended.

"You wannnn drinnnnk?" beckoned another.

"No, no, and no!" I said, throwing my hands out to the sides as we rushed into the main courtyard area. Anne held back a grin.

"You want maaaap sir?" she drawled out.

"No miss, I just want a massaaaage!"

Anne gave in and laughed again. I wanted to push out a few more jokes. But the little girl silenced us both.

"Yes, sir. Massage over there," she replied, pointing to a row of tents in the distance.

This was weird on many levels. There were actual massage tents at the royal palace? And why were tours allowed inside? More to the point, why was the little girl not in school? I was feeling uneasy taking it all in.

The heat was draining me away, which didn't help either. For all our questioning and boat riding preparation, it was already noon by the time we started walking around. The midday sun was mixing well with the humidity to make this all a not so pleasant experience. How did the royals cope? Why would anyone build a palace or capital city in such a hot place? I wondered if I should even ask myself these things. But in doing so, I found myself questioning even the most basic of things, like being highly suspicious of getting cheated by a ten-year-old when buying a coke.

We walked around. Ducking where possible into any shadows to shade from the sun. The palace itself was nearly all gold or painted gold. It meant the searing sun glared and bounced heat all around us at a pronounced level as we walked through the lush gardens. We took some photographs of golden cone spires. Marvelled at the intricate tiny glass tiles. Posed in front of some statues. Gave in to three drink touts and one ice cream tout before making our way out. The next destination was to be a big temple with a giant Buddha lying down. It would have been more impressive if he'd been standing up, but the throng of tourists queuing up to see it seemed to suggest it was still worthwhile.

It was literally a large golden buddha statue lying down. I wondered, briefly, why the Buddha would be lying down. As opposed to sitting up and teaching or meditating or doing what buddhas do. I then went to the feet of the statue where oyster shell inscriptions covered the buddha's feet. In fairness, this bit was impressive.

"Look!" gasped Anne. "Baby Monks! How cute!"

Babies might have been a slight exaggeration. Primary school monks were more like it. But Anne made a good point about being cute. Dressed in bright tangerine robes, the little guys were all lined up and dropping coins into brass jars beside the Buddha statue. A sign of good luck according to one of my photocopies.

"Take a photo of me with a baby monk, will you?"

"Huh?" I replied as Anne's phone was thrust into my hands.

"I'll just stand by one of the jar thingy's and when a baby monk comes by, you snap us, okay? It'll look so cute on my Insta!"

Phone in hand, I made every effort to try to take as natural a photograph as humanly possible. Not easy considering Anne was standing there with a Cheshire cat like frozen grin waiting for a monk to pass by. Her perspiring cleavage had a streak of fake tan running straight down the middle. The other issue was the fact the baby monks didn't stop when they dropped coins into the jars. A monk finally looked up a little as Anne nudged just a bit too close for comfort and ended up scaring him into a mild freeze at the sight of her shiny brown cleavage with melting skin dripping down the middle.

"How's it look?"

I pressed review. Not bad, actually. Well, aside from the fact the young monk was transfixed on her boobs. Better than a cheesy grin photo for sure.

"Aww, they're so cute!"

"Lunch?" I offered to move on before they arrested us for monk harassment.

"Sure, then how about a real massaaage?"

Wow, it felt like first contact. Finally, it looked like our mini war was over. Things were really looking up. Thai food was divine, which helped keep the mood up too. It was also cheap, available everywhere, and seemed to make a good critic out of every tourist in the restaurant. It meant, so long as it was positive, I could actually hold a conversation with Anne over food.

"This Pad Thai has better noodles than the guesthouse last night."

"Uh huh," replied Anne, sucking a long noodle up with her divine lips.

"And, the spring rolls, so crunchy."

"Ohhh, yea." nodded Anne biting down on the small golden roll.

Food has been the missing link to the missing spark in our relationship, it seemed.

***

After lunch, I found myself in the lap of luxury. My first Thai massage. Lying face down on a perfumed towel, the soothing hands of a beautiful Thai girl ran up and down my back. It couldn't get any better.

I'd never had a 'real' massage before. The closest I ever got was from Anne one night back at my flat. She'd bought some oil from a flea market one weekend and wanted to test it out. Aside from an initial third-degree burn after she heated it up. It wasn't too bad. The whole thing ended up with two oily bodies having a shag and making a pair of sheets looking like grease proof paper.

That was about two weeks before the incident that ruined everything.

***

"I love you Anne."

Who'd have thought those four little romantic words would send a woman into an overdrive of hatred towards the one who said them. Granted, it was after some serious, heavy drinking. I'd also just thrown up and forgotten to remove my splattered t-shirt before attempting to kiss her. But the truth is I did, genuinely, at that time, really mean every word.

Like most things in life, I soon discovered what the next morning after an alcohol fuelled night of passion can bring. Apparently I'd thrown up in bed. A rather damp yellow patch with orange and dark bits dotted around my side of the bed proved this to be true. But worse than the embarrassment or thumping headache was Anne's sudden coldness to me after confessing my feelings. I scampered to change the sheets. Apologized as much as any man with a jackhammer pummelling his dehydrated brain could. Yet it all fell on deaf ears.

40

One moment there were hidden rendezvous and overnight stays. The next it was meeting up with Anne and Charles at the pub with her making out like I barely existed. Well, that's what we used to do, anyway. But usually she'd send me a covert look when Charles wasn't paying attention.

This was around the time I started my three times a week run. The belly pinch the week before was part of my motivation. But now, it was also an attempt to show her I was in top shape and taking our upcoming trip seriously. None of this made her bat an eyelid.

I remembered my attempts so well.

"I downloaded a list of the best white sand beaches in Thailand last night."

"Cool," replied Charles. "I bet you'll see some real talent over there, eh?!"

"What'd you think, Anne?" I asked, trying to make some light of everything. "Will it be all hot babes or do you think you'll meet a beach hunk too?"

Anne looked up from her phone, raised her eyes and ignored my attempt at covert humour.

"You've got your work cut out for you there, mate," admonished Charles. "I think Anne's got a list of temples, museums, and the odd local food stall she wants to see first."

As brothers went, Charles was pretty cool. He'd defended his sister all the way through school during her Harry Potter 'Witchy' phase. In University he'd used his first lowly paid job to help pay for a couple of her overseas student exchange clubs. She was his baby nerd sister, and he saw nothing else but that. I valued my life too much to tell him anything else.

Once there was some bloke that started a rumour that Anne was a lesbian because she walked out on a date with him. Charles was nearly kicked out for, allegedly, beating the hell out of him in a University toilet. It wasn't the lesbian accusation that ticked Charles off. It was the fact that the guy spoke badly about her. Anne also confided in me she told Charles the guy had tried it on with her. That was the icing on the cake. There was no proof it was Charles. No one said anything. But the fresh grazes on Charles' hands were a dead giveaway. Suffice it to say, nobody went near Anne for the rest of the year.

"Those Thai guys are not so hot anyway," I said, laughing back a drink self-consciously.

Anne shot me a look through narrowed eyes. What the hell was wrong with her. I only said 'I love you'.

***

"You're an immature, insensitive, wanker."

My ultimate confrontation with Anne was not going to plan. I simply wanted to know why she was so odd with me? So a month before leaving, I called by her house when Charles was out. She wasn't happy that I'd showed up.

"What did I do wrong?"

Silence.

"How can I make it better if you don't tell me?"

More silence.

"Arh," I groaned in exasperation. "I said I'm sorry. What more can I do?"

"Leave."

"Just tell me already? We can't go on like this. We're going to Thailand in four weeks, for fuck's sake?"

"I shouldn't have to tell you."

"Why not? I don't know what I did?"

"You should know."

It was like trying to grasp at invisible clues. So I caved in. "I don't know. I'm thick. I'm stupid. I do not know what I did. And I'm sorry for it ... okay."

Anne looked unimpressed. "You're just looking for too much

commitment, Jonny."

This was the reason she hated me? Commitment? Anne continued to unload her reasons for the silent treatment.

"You're getting too serious about all this. Too caught up in something that isn't there."

I stood there, aghast at Anne's reasoning. Then a second gut punch hit me. She did not love me. It ravaged me on many fronts. First, she hinted we were not a serious couple. We were a couple. What wasn't serious about that? What's wrong with saying what you feel? Even after a few too many.

Second, this was coming from a girl who seemed happiest when I told her things like she was the only one for me. Or that she was the most beautiful girl in the world. Now suddenly I was too committed? It must have been the 'love you' words that had thrown her. I thought that's what she wanted. Commitment and all that. Vodka and red bull. Never again. It brings out too much in me.

"I … I was just …"

"It doesn't matter Jonny," she said coldly, picking up her mobile. "Whatever there was is over now."

My heart sank a little more. I knew she was stubborn and this silent treatment had gone on too long to change her mind at a doorstop. I nodded and put on the best sad eyed look I could. It wasn't hard.

"Okay. Fair enough. I'm sorry."

There was an awkward silence.

"Hug goodbye?"

She looked up from her phone. Paused. Then nodded. It was an icy embrace. In fact, I could have had something viral from the distance she kept between our bodies during that farewell hug. Then, just for a fleeting moment as we pulled away, I could have sworn I felt her hands open up on my back and give me a gentle rub. And that was that. Just friends again.

***

A warm pair of hands slid down my back and stroked the side of my rib cage tenderly on the way back up. The Thai massage was indeed a wonderful thing.

"Nearly donnnne," purred the masseuse. "You turn over, sir."

I must have nearly dozed off as I felt as if my whole body was in a near twilight condition. I was so relaxed it nearly felt like I didn't have a care in the world. That is, until I turned over and realized my penis was alive and rigidly confused at all the tender care my body was now getting.

Holding onto the towel, I paused in mid-turn. But the girl, in all innocence and with a beautiful Thai smile, merely held my hips with her hands and gently helped me complete the turn before turning away to place some more oil on her hands. Turning back, she gave a pouty look at the hands-free mini-tent that I had inadvertently created with the towel. She went from pouty to a wide smile with ease. Anne was in the next room. I suddenly felt the world speed up.

CHAPTER 6

A TRUCE

Kao San Road at night beats to a livelier drum than during the heat of the day. The air is just 'hot' outside as opposed to feeling like you are being cooked from both the inside and outside. Bright neon tubes flash calling signs for bars, clubs, money exchangers, and something to do with donkey bongs. The touts also seem a fraction smarter at night. Their smiles are brighter, and prices often come down to 'free'. Which means you avoid those places and opt to pay for your drinks. Everything seemed a little easier too. With that revelation, I suddenly had a slight, and I do mean slight, like for Thailand at last.

"What's say we hit up the places with fewer blokes wearing footy shirts?"

Anne nodded in agreement with me before stopping by a young Thai guy in a blue Nike t-shirt selling Lonely Planets. She flicked through one as the Thai guy remained curiously silent while nuzzling a faded Thailand guidebook into her hands.

"You think we should?"

"Dunno," I said, peering at the book. I remembered Stuart saying they were fake. And automated these days. But the Thailand one Anne was thumbing through looked pretty legit. I still favoured my photocopies.

"How much?" I asked.

"Only eight hundred baaaht," quoted the Thai guy whilst pulling out a plastic bag to pack it away before we'd even said yes.

"Aw come on," shrugged Anne. "That's too much. How about five?"

The guy put the plastic bag down and looked disgusted.

"I don't think he's happy."

"Shut up Jonny."

Anne held up five fingers.

"My photocopies are cheaper." I protested.

"Jonny," snapped Anne. "You're not helping! Five hundred."

The guy shook his head. Then looked away as if we'd insulted his children.

"F i v e … H u n d r e d … *Baaaaaht*," Anne replied in her best Thai accent.

The little drawn out *baaaaaht* bit at the end was quite impressive and close to the local way of saying it. Again, the guy shook his head. I was wondering what Anne would try next.

"Fuck it," cursed Anne, turning away. "Let's go get a pint."

No sooner had we taken one step away when the little guy barked at us.

"Six hundred … LAST."

"Done!"

***

We sat at a table on a bar's balcony overlooking Kao San Road and made a beer toast after a good flick through our newfound guidebook.

"To the conquering heroes." I toasted.

Chink.

"To cheap booze!"

Chink.

"To cheap massaaaages."

Anne let out a laugh and exhaled. "If only I could get that sort of treatment back home."

I nodded, shuffled my legs a little, and changed the conversation. "What do you want to do tomorrow? More temples?"

"Dunno really," Anne paused. She bit her lower lip and frowned a little. "I really liked the little baby monks today. But that massage I had was unreal. So relaxing, don't you think?"

Again, I nodded in agreement and let her continue on without bringing up anything about my own.

"I could do with some more of that, I think. Eight months of dreary England, Uni, and rain. It's time for some pampering."

"I used to give you good massages."

There was an immediate, awkward silence. I cursed myself for bringing it up. Just as things were relaxing. Anne's smile dropped, and she looked down at our table.

"Don't start it up, Jonny," she breathed deeply. "Just drop it."

Her genuine tone took me aback. As if she was truly tired of the fighting. Perhaps a truce was indeed in order. Putting my glass down, I nodded in submission.

"No problem."

Another shorter silence followed until I broke it. "How about some shots to wash away the past?"

Anne looked up. Scrunched her mouth up and then mouthed the words 'Let's do it'.

"Let's partay!!"

We hit the bar upstairs, running. Two shots of tequila before moving onto mango inspired Thai cocktails. We finally toasted to the end of Uni. Then it was onto something to eat which was easy as the bar also sold wicked Thai food from spicy chicken wings, to thai style chilli pizza, and even British style chips with some sort of chilli ketchup. I never knew Thai food could taste so similar to food back home. The promise of a long Thai massaaaage in the morning to recover from our impending night on the town only added to our enjoyment.

We moved downstairs where there was air-conditioning that kept things deliciously cool. It was lit up with spotlights and neon signs in every nook and cranny. It meant everything and everyone was on show.

White guys from the UK, America and various unidentifiable European nations were predominant and all chilling out like it was the best place on earth. Maybe they all got free holidays instead of apartment deposits from their parents? I wondered if the parents knew where their money was going. And why was nearly everyone white? I spotted one black guy at a table with a Thai girl. Everyone else seemed to be white. Was this a thing to do with Thailand? Bangkok? Or was there some other social meaning to it? It wasn't an age thing either; it seemed.

Dotted around the room were tall tables and stools that had an assortment of beer-bellied middle-aged men with Thai girlfriends sitting around them. In the middle area were small round tables with matching chairs that had either younger tourist couples sitting alone or in occasional mini-groups when the tables were pushed closer. In-between all this were even more young white guys standing around in groups with Thai girlfriends of all ages and, to be fair, sizes joining in on their conversations. Another odd thing about all this was that not one tourist girl had a Thai boyfriend. They all seemed to have a boyfriend from back home with them. And no girls seemed to be in a group together either. It seemed Bangkok was the place to be for a horny white male, no matter his body type, age or how badly he dressed.

We watched a group of Australian guys do beer bongs near the front window until their stomachs couldn't take any more liquid. The savvy Thai bar girls had buckets at the ready, with one tattooed older girl keeping her hand on an actual mop and bringing it out whenever things went awry. It was all so normal for Thailand; it seemed. Including when the most inebriated of these guys had a bevvy of Thai girls descend on them as the night went on. The girls helped them back into chairs and offered gentle shoulder rubs in exchange for a drink, a walk outside, or a flat out tip. It was literally like a well-oiled business.

"Gawd how old is she?"

Anne pointed to a strange-looking older guy with a mat of wet badly dyed black hair at one of the tall tables. He was at least seventy but dressed like a young hip hop artist going through some mid-life crises. He even wore a large metal chain around his neck with a big pendant. And he didn't seem to care. Perhaps it was the seriously young looking Thai girl with him in yellow hot pants that distracted him. She seemed to laugh at everything he said to her.

"Eighteen …" I said, cringing at my optimism.

Anne winced. "I dunno Jonny. Seriously, that's some fucked up shit. She looks younger. Wayyyy younger."

"She's twenty-five."

We both turned as a tall blond guy in his thirties leaned into our conversation with an all-knowing grin. "Sorry," he continued. "Couldn't help looking last week myself. His names Derrick. Swedish I think. They've been together for a few years now. Harmless."

"You know him?" asked Anne.

"Naw, I just remember asking the same thing when I arrived."

The blond guy introduced himself as he ordered a beer. Steve was from Perth in Australia and on his annual pilgrimage to Thailand for a month on the beaches. He was also one of the few Australians, either not completely pissed or attached to a Thai girl. On the final few days of his holiday, Steve was just out for a couple of beers with some people from his guesthouse. Not a bad group to get invited to join in with.

"I'm not sure if that's a ladyboy or not?" nodded one of Steve's mates towards a couple by the bar as we joined them.

"Transgender!" corrected another.

"Mate," replied the first. "It's Thailand. You're not in bloody Sydney. Nobody cares about your fifty gender identifying types here."

"Yea," added a younger guy wearing an 'I Love Dallas' t-shirt. "It's way more relaxed over here than back home."

We were a mix of newcomers and long-term pros finishing up their backpacking tours of South East Asia. The latter talked about the incredible beaches in southern Thailand as if they were true places of paradise once lost but found again by them. Turquoise crystal clear water. Remote tropical islands surrounded by pristine white sand beaches. Whether you wanted to party or chill out, it seemed Southern Thailand was the place to go. We listened to them like little newborns taking it all in. We were learning about Thailand from the people that had travelled through it, around it, and back into it again.

"Try going south to Ko Pha Ngan if you want to escape all the Bangkok hassle," suggested Steve.

"Damn, Ko Pha Ngan," sighed a Belgium guy with a knowing nod. "Outstanding full moon party."

"Freaking Ace!" blurted another.

"Ko Pha Na…" I stumbled.

"Ko Pha NNNgan, mate," corrected Steve. "White sand beaches. Cheap digs. Party all night or chill out on a quiet stretch. Go climb a mountain. Have a full moon party every month. Whatever … Ko Pha Ngan has got it all. Even a monastery if you want to volunteer there."

Anne's interest suddenly picked up. "A monastery and a full moon party every month?"

"Yea, instead of once a year, some enterprising locals made it a monthly thing. Nice, eh!"

A round of claps, cheers and foot-stomping took place.

I looked over at Anne. "Interested?"

"If I can have a massage like today down there, hell yeah!"

CHAPTER 7

THE ISLAND

As hangovers go Thai, hangovers were not that bad. I think it had something to do with no alarm clocks, work, university, or any combination of these being the main reasons. By two o'clock we were already up and wondering how anyone could work in the all-engulfing big city heat Bangkok produced. Anne, as promised, disappeared off for her mid 'morning' massage. I thought about it. Seriously thought about it. But forewent one until later to Skype Charles and let him know our plans. Who knows if we'll have internet in Ko Pha Ngan.

It was only our third day in Bangkok, and I was already making friends along Kao San Road. Or at least people recognised me. The fried banana lady outside our guesthouse automatically held up the same number of bananas on sticks I'd eaten the day before for breakfast.

Bing-Bong.

The 7-11 was now becoming a part of Bangkok's natural order of background noise. Further down the road and the bookseller held up the same Thailand book we bought from him the day before. And inside our bar, Steve gave me a wave from his table as I settled down with my laptop for a morning/afternoon of planning. Yes, settling in was indeed the right word.

The free Wi-Fi was working, but just not good enough to Skype. So I wrote Charles a quick message to let him know about our plans.

That done, I sent my parents an email.

Hi Mum & Dad,

Anne and I are having a great time here. Everything's so easy but so hot. We spent yesterday at the Grand Palace and a Buddha temple. We even got to spend time with young Monks in training!

Tomorrow we're going to a beach in Southern Thailand to check out the snorkelling and maybe even a little kite flying!

Anyway, I've got to go now. I have to buy the bus tickets. I will email you soon.

Love you both,
Jonny.

P.S. Dad, remember to worm the dogs!

For the next hour, I drank iced coffee, ate pancakes and posted some photos from yesterday at the palace on Instagram. The thought of doing all this on a beach seemed even more blissful. Anne arrived waving a big envelope in one hand, and a dog-eared book in the other.

"I got the tickets!"

"Huh?"

"The tickets to Ko Pha Ngan, you phlegm. The masseuse from this morning has a brother that works as a travel agent. I scored us direct bus tickets. And … boat tickets to the island."

"What island?"

"Ko Pha Ngan? Where do you think?"

"It's an island? I thought it was a beach?"

Steve saved me.

"So you lads are off, then?"

Anne wiggled into a chair and gave two small thumbs up. "Can't wait! I even picked up this book for the ride down there."

I stared at an upside-down picture of Leonardo DiCaprio. Then picked it up to read the back cover. The book was well-read and the back cover had certainly seen better days. Something about a guy who discovers a paradise island in southern Thailand. Looks like we were living the dream.

"Let me give you the name of a good place to stay." Steve opened up the cover of the book and wrote a note. "They've got fan and air-con rooms. Only about six hundred or eight hundred baht. If you call them tonight, they'll even pick you up when you arrive."

"Really," cooed Anne.

"Yea, really," laughed Steve. "Don't worry, it's not like here. They'll look after you down there. Anyway, gotta go buy some souvenirs and stuff for back home. Catcha later guys."

I had to admit I was pretty pleased with the turn of events over the past forty-eight hours. I'd gone from the blame boy of misery in paradise. To actually have Anne talking to me again, and soon we'd be on an actual paradise island. Things just couldn't get any better! Well, they could. Knowing it might be a while. I joined Anne for one last massage at the same place as yesterday. I figured they mightn't have that sort of thing on a remote 'island'.

***

My good fortune continued. I had been expecting the overnight bus trip to Ko Pha Ngan to be a nightmare, let alone the ferry crossing. Thailand isn't exactly known for its safety measures. I had to physically restrain myself from Googling any more about car crashes and ferry sinkings in Thailand. In truth, a minivan picked us up at the guesthouse. Drove us to a larger station. Transferred us to a huge two-tier pink bus with reclining seats, air-con, and even a free mini bottle of water. Maybe Thai hospitality was all about getting off the tourist trail.

Anne spent the first half of the night reading The Beach. She put it down at the end of every chapter to let me know what happened. Each time I stirred awake from a perpetual doze. But my nods worked and I think she appreciated the time I spent looking interested in her chapter spoilers. By the middle of the night, the bus was full of young backpackers. Some trying to sleep like me. Others flapped about with maps and guidebooks while a few brought drinks and decided nobody should get a proper night's sleep. Privately, I hoped not a single one was going to Ko Pha Ngan, nor even heard about it.

By morning, they shuffled us off the bus and rounded us up before two Thai men led us, and about a dozen others, to a ferry dock. It was a two-hour wait there because of some delay involving a capsized boat, which had me anxiously texting mum and dad about how much I missed them. After that, I got into the swing of sending a barrage of Instagram posts about the two old ladies selling bananas wrapped in dried coconut at the dock. There wasn't much else to do other than melt away in the heat. The others either slept or were trying to pick up a signal on their phones like me. The ferry itself was a breeze and at the other end, true to their word, were a different pair of Thai guys waiting from the Red Mango Lodge. We sent Steve from the bar in Bangkok a selfie with two thumbs up from the back of their pickup truck.

Best of all, similar men carted everyone else off in different directions. I could feel the tension fade from my shoulders, knowing we were indeed going to our own private paradise. The men confirmed it. We were going to the quieter side of the island that offered everything the other side did, only better. A town separated both sides. Which we passed through in all of four seconds. We were really in the sticks, it seemed!

By mid-afternoon, we had our feet up outside our bamboo

cottage slash hut overlooking the most beautiful white beach I'd ever seen.

"Paradise," I said, sipping on a straw from a rum cocktail inside a green coconut. "Absolute bloody paradise."

Anne stretched back and threw her fully read in under twenty-four hours copy of The Beach on the table separating our two beds. "I still can't believe a place like this exists."

"And we've got three entire months of places like this!"

"Just under," replied Anne. "But it's a good start. Mind my stuff, will you? I'm going to test out the waters."

Dropping her towel, Anne showed off her two-piece swimsuit for the first time. A dark green affair with little gold loops on either hip and one right in the middle of her cleavage. I felt my thoughts wandering to places they were once permitted. Quickly, I sat up, shaking my head. The heat, the booze, and the idea of being in paradise were causing me to think like I was sixteen again.

I didn't seem to be alone in my thoughts, either. Even though we were staying on the quiet side of the island, there was still a fair bit of daylight romance going on. The cottage next to us had one very tanned guy who was with an equally tanned blond girl. They appeared once, briefly, only to look out at the sea before darting back inside again.

To our right was yet another couple in a similar cottage. Only they hadn't come up for air yet. Judging from the odd shriek and giggle, they didn't seem to be in too much of a rush, either. Then there was the beach. Golden white, clean and picturesque. There were a few enormous umbrellas and a couple of makeshift banana leaf wind barriers that protected suntanning bodies from the most intense of the sun's rays. Directly ahead were two girls lying flat out in the sun. The photogenic tropical surroundings enhanced their bodies. I suddenly felt lonely and horny at the same time.

"What's up?"

It was Anne. She was back from her brief cooling-off dip and was glistening with tantalising wet drops of seawater running down her long body. I shook my head again and tried to forget about the raging torrent of hormones coursing through my body.

"Nothing," I said, sitting up even further to hide any potentially embarrassing situations. "Just taking in the sights."

"Wicked," she said, bouncing buoyantly down into her chair on the porch. "What say we head out early and check out the town or village or whatever they like it to be known? I'm kinda still cramped up from the overnight bus."

"Sound's like a plan …"

Two young European looking guys sporting matching pink t-shirts and strange-looking orange tans interrupted us. They were handing out leaflets.

> *Half Moon Party on Haad Rin Beach!!!*
> *FREE pick up by The Pink Fish Bar!*
> *Happy Hour 2nd drinks FREE! Last until sunrise and get a free breakfast special!*

"You guys just arrive?" asked the taller one.

"Yep."

"Excellent," beamed the shorter. "I'm Matt, and that's Jeff. We're from the Pink Fish Bar. You guys need your own pick-up tonight?"

"Eh …" I shot a look at Anne, "We're kinda beat from the bus last night. Just wanted an early night."

"No worries," exclaimed the shorter one, who I think was Matt, as he put a leaflet under our water bottles. "It's a free pickup. If you want to come back early, just let me know and we can put you on one of the minivans heading out on a round to collect people."

Anne shrugged and gave a brief nod.

"What time ..."

"Pick you up about seven," interrupted Jeff. "On the main road just outside of the entrance here. See you then!"

The two guys moved on in unison towards a sleeping couple on the beach. It seemed we had just sealed our fates for the night.

CHAPTER 8

THE PARTAY ...

Who'd have thought a beach could be lit up like New Year's Eve and sound like a warehouse nightclub at the same time. Apparently, the guys at the Pink Fish Bar knew the secret. Insert four giant ear drum annihilation speakers the size of compact cars in a squared-off area of a beach. Turn the volume to maximum and the bass as low as possible. Place the bar in front of the speakers with swinging coloured spotlights and have local girls in tiny denim shorts and pink t-shirts serve ice-cold beer. Done deal. It sold me.

Dinner was free, too. A bowl of fish drowned in coconut milk mixed with rum on a bed of soft Thai rice. I'd have gladly passed out then and there if it wasn't for the vodka red bulls I'd switched to after dinner. They were at half price. One-eighth of the price compared to back home. Wherever that was. These manage to both inebriate me and keep me feeling like a barista who sampled every coffee they sent out. Adding to this was the deafening thud thud thud of Baby D's techno music that had most of our table's conversation starting with 'What?' And 'say again?'

Anne was even more lively than me after dinner. "This really happens every night?"

"Every Friday," shouted a yellow bikini glad girl next to her.

"Every night they only bring out two speakers."

I couldn't hear a thing. But the fact there was a girl in a yellow bikini talking made me want to try.

"What?"

"Two speakers." The girl yelled, holding up a finger on each hand.

"No, there's four, isn't there?"

"Four what?" shouted back a topless bloke with a Maui shoulder tattoo.

"Four speakers!" yelled the girl beside him.

Ordinarily, this would have been maddening. But on Haad Rin Beach it was normal. Haad Rin Beach was basically the Pink Fish Bar's private area on the island. Well, so long as the owner paid the appropriate fees to the island administration. It meant anything could happen here and nobody would complain.

We couldn't help but smile, toast the epic weekly event and join in the bar games that the pink t-shirted duo of Matt and Jeff began. Most of the games involved crawling up race tracks marked out in the sand. Either with a member of the opposite sex on your shoulders, back, or in two cases dragged by the ankles. The winners got free shots of some local firewater drink, after which they never won a race again.

The Pink Fish's methodology was simple. Get the punters hot and panting as much as possible so they'd buy more drinks. It worked a charm. By one a.m. the beat lowered slightly and changed into the best of the decades' top hits. Two campfires sprung up on the sand between the bar and the sea. They dedicated one campfire to the daredevil crowd. It was all simple stuff, like spinning a bottle and daring one person from different couples, or a single, into the sea, stripping each other naked, and coming back wearing each other's clothes. It was fun to watch and energetic. But we were both still pretty tired from the overnight bus, so we chose the chill out campfire further away from the bar.

"You want a spliff?"

I turned to Jeff, who was in charge of our campfire, as he extended out his hand holding a joint. It had been a while since I'd smoked anything. Now seemed like a good time to relax back.

"Sure."

If there was a place made for letting loose the years of pent up studentship, then I think we'd found it. The joint fizzled as I inhaled deeply, counted to five and enjoyed the world, getting all fuzzy. My worries washed away and a giant uncontrollable grin pushed my lips back.

Anne took the joint as I exhaled. "Good?"

"Fuck yeah," I said in some strange, echoing manner. "This is one good hit."

She drew in the smoke and held it longer than me before finally exhaling. I had the feeling Anne was well used to smoking weed. Something I'd never noticed before. Maybe the Harry Potter school girl had been holding onto even more secrets during her school days than anyone knew. She took another drag before handing it back.

"Hey Jonny," Jeff said, coming closer to me. "You want something a little stronger?"

"Like what?"

"Indigo Dream."

"Dunno, I think we're doing alright."

"Yea," continued Jeff. "But they work wonders for the last dance."

"Last dance?"

"Yea mate. The Last Dance. It's when we turn up the beat for one last hour to celebrate the moon."

I looked up to see a thin sliver of moon. "Bit small isn't it?"

"No mate. It's to celebrate the half-moon party coming next week. You know, giving thanks in advance and all that. It's a local thing."

I felt something being placed down in the sand by my pocket. "No worries mate," smiled Jeff. "Try one, if you don't like it, no problem."

"Uh … Okay, thanks."

"I put one in there for your girl too," he said, winking at me. A small white and blue pill appeared briefly between his teeth before he washed it down with a drink. He then stood up and shouted over to the other campfire. "Ten minutes to the last dance!"

I'd never taken anything stronger than a spliff before in my life. Well, there was one night of E but I was sure it was fake. I thought about it for a minute while Jeff skipped to the bar. He seemed to do okay with it. We were also far away from home. Free from everything. I was actually considering it despite something niggling at me to not be stupid.

"What's that?"

Anne saw me playing with the little plastic bag and I swore under my breath. "Indigo …" I paused, trying to remember. "Indigo Dream."

"Fuck me, where'd you score that? That shits hot."

"How do you know?"

Anne, deadpan, ignored me. It was one of those do or die moments where you just know you are at a crossroads in life. It didn't matter how or why Anne could possibly know what an Indigo Dream was. Or if she's had one before. What mattered was that we were at a crossroads, together.

"Emmm, you want one?"

The music level suddenly thrashed to new heights, and the spotlights started up again. With both campfires blazing high into the sky and the sea churning away in front of us, it seemed like a grand mix of modern life mixing with primal instincts.

The sand vibrated to the beat of the music as a Thai fire swinger came out to start the dance with a spectacular display. Set on long metal chains, she swung two flaming balls around and around with her hands. The fire left trails in the dark night sky and we shouted out in appreciation. Jeff and Matt needed little to get the crowd going.

We were all caught up in the rapture of our newfound freedom.

We danced and danced. Arms in the air and heads bopping up and down. Tiredness was nowhere to be found, and it didn't matter who anybody was. We just danced in the cool sea air to the beat of whatever. I loved every minute of it. Jumping to the beat and throwing my hands into the air, I briefly lost balance in the sand. A blond girl from the other campfire nearly toppled over in the brief collision. We steadied ourselves with an embrace. She smiled up at me and grabbed both my hands to the beat of the music. I let out a whoooo! And she laughed out loud.

Before I knew it, I was dancing some hybrid version of the Macarena with a bikini blond from who knows where. I held on to her hips , spun her around, and pulled her close to mimic her dance moves. Then I felt another set of hands on my waist. Anne. We were forming a dancing chain.

"Whoo, whoo," we chanted as we snaked along the beach.

Playing follow the leader, we circled the bar before going down into the sea, clothes and all. The dance train broke up as people lost balance and fell over in a chorus of laughs and cheers. I lost my grip on the blond in front of me as I tumbled over to the side with a splash into the sea. Instinctively, I jumped up again as the water covered my body. Then I turned to see Anne struggling to sit up beside me.

"Anne!" I shouted in my best heroic tone, reaching down to pull her up with both hands.

Water ran off Anne's head and down her top as she wiped the excess from her face.

"Jonny?"

I pulled her closer, and our eyes locked together. Memories came flooding back.

Her eyes changed from panic to hunger, and she pulled me into her lips. At long last, we were together again.

Our days along the beach comprised waking up about noon. Ordering a breakfast of mangoes and pancakes with coffee outside on the porch of our cottage. We followed this with a quick dip in the sea, which was then followed by a smoke of the local good stuff and a siesta. Intermingled in all this were occasional hot, steamy sessions of Anne sex. Of which I was truly addicted. And had been for quite a while. Well, prior to saying those words. I will never say them again.

This time, however, sex with Anne wasn't quite the same. Not for my will to try. It was when and where she wanted it. Normally, this wouldn't bother anyone who wasn't having sex. The mere thought of sex at the whim of another can indeed be a turn on. Unless you were also noticing other girls on the beach, too. And they were noticing you. It meant I could have other opportunities. Not that I was interested. But I was aware of this recent phenomenon and even more aware of it whenever Anne turned me down. This was definitely new to me. Was it Thailand? Or was it the fact I was more relaxed here? Or something else? I couldn't work it out. I just knew it was something new that was provoked whenever she would have a go at me.

"You stink. Take a shower" was her usual morning excuse. Then when I'd come out of the bathroom, she'd be out having a swim. One morning, I actually woke up first and snuck off for a shower. It made no difference.

"Gawwwd my head hurts," she'd groan. "Get lost, Jonny."

It wasn't like she wasn't a morning person or anything. One night, we stayed up all night at the Pink Fish and had a beach session as the sun came up. Sadly, that ended up with two more days of no sex as she complained the sand had made her bits all sore. All the same, I wasn't complaining.

More of a moan. At least we were getting on well again. Though, wellish seemed a better word.

It helped that Jeff kept everyone happy with a regular supply of cheap weed. He never dealt at the Pink Fish or Haad Rin Beach. He'd always bring it down to our beach or to our cottage. Thailand has some fairly strict drug laws and so long as he kept his business away from public meeting places, the local police left him and us alone.

We saved the blue indigo for Fridays nights or the quarter, dark, and half-moon parties. By the end of our first week, we had made more friends than we did throughout our time at university. Most people came to stay a week but ended up staying for weeks. One guy from Sweden gave up his flight to Borneo just because it clashed with the upcoming half moon party.

The only thing that was missing, according to Anne, were the temples and monks that she'd loved in Bangkok. So we took a day trip away from the island with some others to the mainland and visited the local monastery, where you could volunteer if you wanted to. Something I was quite keen on Anne not doing. So I went along to make sure she wouldn't get distracted by teaching baby monks English or the like.

Jeff and Matt had put together the cultural trip and a few others from Ko Pha Ngan joined us. It wasn't all bad. The monastery was actually fairly huge and, unlike the places in Bangkok, completely devoid of tourists. Inside there was a colourful Buddha statue at the rear of the building. People in Thailand prayed while sitting on the carpeted floor instead of in a pew. The main building had large doors on three sides that let in gusts of warm air from the outside, making it all seem larger than it actually was. The tidy gardens around the monastery were a mix of hedgerows, a small pond, a few tall trees and wooden benches. A few monks tended to various colourful flowers, while others sat under trees in the shade. It wasn't exactly a 'happening place', but it made a pleasant change to our daily beach routine. Thankfully, we saw nothing about volunteering there either. I think even Anne found it a 'once is enough' type of place.

"Do you think the Monks smoke weed?"

"What?" Anne glared at me as we walked back to the main town area by the dock.

"Not the baby monks!" I stated in horror, "I mean the older chilled out ones."

"No, of course not Jonny," she replied. "They're monks, you know."

"Right."

Matt and Jeff had warned everyone not to take any joints out to the mainland, as the local police were fond of nicking backpackers passing through. Most were hassled for an on the spot 'fine'. But apparently, a few were actually taken downtown and charged. The stories of Thai jails were a terrible side to Thailand. Something we used to scare the newcomers around the campfires with. The police never showed up on our island. That agreement between them and the bar owners kept us safe.

"I mean, don't they get bored?" I continued as we walked down the town's main street. "I mean, what do they do all day? Meditate. Eat rice. Meditate. Sleep. Meditate. Ring a bell ... Weed would help them pass the day a bit faster wouldn't it?"

"They're trying to find their Zen," sighed Anne, as if she knew what she was talking about.

"Their what?"

"Their Zen," she repeated. Anne had read a book on Buddhism left behind by another guest back at Haad Rin Beach and was quickly rebooting her Harry Potter ways again. "It's like the highest level of spirituality you can reach."

She paused before correcting herself. "It's the path to enlightenment, you know? You're at peace with everyone and everything."

"Yea," I joked. "So they can light one up and get there a bit faster, eh?"

"Asshole."

I sat outside a local bar as Anne and a group of the others went in while we waited for the ferry to take us back. She had a point about my joke. I was pushing it a bit far. But I was really enjoying life these days. It was so relaxed and chilled. There was no reason to always get so uptight or worry about things. I only came this far to keep her happy. Sitting around watching a bunch of monks in robes hit big gongs once every hour really didn't appeal to me. I got it, but it just wasn't my thing.

The bar was a local half-outside, half-inside affair. There was a nice breeze, so I was glad I didn't follow the others inside. An old Thai woman brought out an ice-cold can of Tiger beer before leaving me alone to the sound of monks hitting gongs in the distance. It was late afternoon, and no one was around. I sighed and thought about what it would be like to stay longer in a place like this.

Things were going well back at Haad Rin Beach. We were old-timers there now. Most people came and stayed for two weeks. We'd been there just over three by now. Noobs straight off the ferry would ask us questions about everything from how to find beach romance to where to get some weed. Girls, in particular, were easy to impress. Never in my life did I ever have a circle of five beach attired girls surround me at a campfire at night hanging on to my every word. Not in my wildest dreams. Well, now they are part of my dreams, but they were no longer my wildest.

Next week, Matt was planning on going to Cambodia for a visa run. It's how he and Jeff stayed so long. Every few months, just before their Thai visa would run out, one of them would take a couple of days off. Catch a bus to the border. Get stamped out. Stay a night in Cambodia, then come back to Thailand the next day. I'd been there so long, Matt asked if I could help to round up noobs for the next half-moon party. I was moving up the island hierarchy, and it felt good.

Reaching down, I pulled out the remnants of a half-smoked spliff from my left sock and lit it up. I smiled. This was my way of enhancing my Zen, I thought as I inhaled. I was sure the monks must have indulged, too. I exhaled and felt a rush come over me. Those university years seemed so far in the past. The grey rainy days of crowded public buses stinking of damp people were a mere afterthought. The only thing that linked me to the past was Anne. We were sleeping together again and yet she still showed no public displays of affection. I'd work on it though. Not like before. This time I was going to go slowly. Reintroduce her to my charm and good wit. We were an established couple on the island, and that was good enough for now. I squinted up at the blue sky, thinking of my plan of action later in the evening. I blew out a series of smoke rings and smiled as they floated away.

"What you got?!"

I spun around to see an angry man wearing sunglasses in a dark brown and tight Thai police uniform pointing directly at me. My stomach flopped and I nearly let its contents fly out as I stood to attention on legs that no longer felt so sturdy.

CHAPTER 9

THE BUST AND THE BUST UP

I did my best to casually drop the small nub of smouldering evidence through my fingers and then scrunch it into non-existence with my foot. Unfortunately, the angry Thai police officer was far too serious to even contemplate finishing such a move. I felt my leg tremble and my ego collapse simultaneously. With one hand moving towards his holstered revolver, he pointed to the still smoking spliff on the ground. Then he hissed louder than I think I've ever heard someone hiss. It was well and truly 'game over'.

I stood there rigid. Every project, homework, and clean up your room excuse flew through my mind to get out of this. Nothing came close. The thought of making a run for it was nowhere to be found. The Thai police officer might have had a potbelly, but he also had a gun. I'd never been this close to a gun before in my life. All I could think about were the American cops all over the news for being trigger-happy. I was sure in the back of nowhere in Thailand this guy would have no problem in using it and also getting away with it. There was also the fear of a Thai prison running through me. Those nights around the island campfire telling stories were now haunting me. All I could muster was a meek whimper that must have sounded like a gerbil having an orgasm.

"You smoke *weeeeed!*" the cop said in that long pronounced Thai fashion while waving at me to step back before squatting down to pick up the evidence. Taking the joint between his fingers, he brought it to his nose and sniffed at the thin line of smoke still emanating from it.

"Weeeeed!" He exclaimed in bizarre surprise again. "You move to the wall." His eighties style police sunglasses hid any hint of emotion. He had a few wrinkles on his shiny face that showed he was not new to the job. This was no rookie, and I was the noob criminal.

Flashes of being cuffed and thrown into a seedy Thai jail crossed my mind again as I continued to back up. Who'd know what happened here? I suddenly thought of the TV series Banged Up Abroad or something. Gritty old tattooed men locked away for years over a small bag of hashish. Crooked cops looking for big bribes planted some of these bags. No lawyers, no calls. Just banged up and forgotten about for years. For the first time since primary school, I just wanted to call out to my mother for help. I just so desperately wanted this man to go away!

"You come with me now," snapped the police officer.

"I … I … I don't know what it is." A feeble excuse. The only one I could muster.

"You come now!"

"I found it on the ground."

"You come."

"I thought it was a cigarette."

"You come now!"

Either he didn't speak English or didn't care. Either way, he was losing his patience. The sunglasses came off and were folded into his top pocket. Then his hand moved back towards his gun.

"You turn … wall. NOW!"

Shit, he was going to cuff me. I gulped down a breath of air and felt the world getting darker. This could not be happening. I turned slowly and then felt a sudden push as I went flat up against the warm, gritty concrete wall of the bar.

"You got gun?"

"No!" I gasped dryly. "No. Look, I'm sorry, it was a mistake. Honest."

A hand patted down my waist and lower back. Then it pulled my shoulder around and I was face to face with the Thai police officer. So close I could see the yellow stains lining his teeth. So close I could see the tiny red veins in his eyes. So close I could do nothing but breathe in his putrid coffee breath. I felt nauseous. I felt my body shiver involuntarily. Then I panicked that the cop could also see this. I was genuinely scared.

"Jonny?" a voice called out in the distance.

The police officer stepped back to look behind him while keeping one hand on my chest. It was Matt, jogging over alone.

"Matt!" I gasped. "Thank fuck, Matt. I'm in real shit here."

"Officer Prapawat," Matt said, ignoring me. "Sawa dee Kaa."

What followed next were a series of grunts and repeated Thai greetings from Matt. I stayed silent and only once during all this did Matt even acknowledge my existence. This was when Officer Prapawat held up the remains of my joint. Matt threw me a vicious look of disbelief and disappointment at my all-knowing stupidity.

More hushed words took over as Matt calmed officer Prapawat down enough to step away from me. I did not move from my spot. All I could think of was that, by the grace of my loosening bowels, Matt could persuade the man that this was all a stupid tourists mistake. That I was an idiot. Perhaps even mentally challenged. Was due to leave tomorrow. And my dear old grandmother was on her deathbed wanting one last visit from her mentally challenged grandson. Anything would do, Matt, anything …

There were longer sentences spoken between Matt and officer Prapawat. None of which I could hear clearly from their distance and hushed tones. With a frown, Matt eventually came over to me.

No longer was he the carefree party maker we relied on. He was now looking more serious than I'd ever seen.

"Five hundred dollars," he whispered.

"Huh?" I replied, failing in my mental capacity to understand the obvious.

Matt looked at me with emboldened eyes to confirm, "Five hundred dollars to make this go away … now."

"Yes, no problem. It's back at the cottage. In my backpack."

Matt looked even harder at me and grimaced. Not in a nice way, either. "Pay it now. It's an on-the-spot fine," he paused, then moved closer to my ear. "Otherwise mate, you are completely fucked!"

"I don't have it here," I blurted honestly. "I've everything back on the island."

Another rush of panic came over me. How could I have left it there? Wait. Wasn't that the right thing to do? It was. Wait, I'm still the idiot here for doing the wrong thing. My mind was tumbling out of control.

Stepping back, Matt scratched at his chin and nodded at Officer Prapawat who did nothing but look over at our group who were coming out of the bar to see what the fuss was about. Anne was at the front.

You'd think getting caught with a joint would boost your standing in terms of bravado.

"You did what??!"

Not true.

While Matt explained what had happened, I got nothing but pissed off stares from the group. Even from the folk who had only arrived a few days ago. Anne's look was the worst. A never-ending glare that bored into me like I was the worst human on the planet.

Matt huddled everyone together. Excluding me. There were some sighs, protests, and a lot of hushed profanity. Then, a pause of silence. Finally, some of the group, including Anne, rummaged through daypacks, wallets, money belts and passports to forage together enough dollar notes to pay my 'on-the-spot fine'. We made it, with fifty to spare. Matt took that as an extra for Prapawat.

Time started to move slowly again. I started to hear by heartbeat inside my chest. Matt and officer Prapawat walked away from us. We all waited a few long minutes in silence. Then, when Matt signalled us to leave for the boat, I knew it was over. Officer Prapawat never turned back to watch us leave. Nobody said anything.

As we loaded ourselves into the boat, relief poured over me. It was over. I tried to break the awkward silence.

"Thanks, everyone, that was a close one!"

I got a few nods, but nothing more. Anne didn't even look at me. I promised to pay everyone once I got back to our cabin. One person nodded with a dismissive head turn. I felt a little put out. I'd just survived a major Thai incident with an armed Thai cop who we had to bribe. Surely that was worth some serious street credit? I followed up by offering the first round of drinks tonight. Nobody replied. For some reason, I had really pissed everyone off.

***

"You'll need to leave tomorrow."

I looked at Jeff in mild confusion and non-sensical understanding. After paying everyone back. And, buying two bottles of beer for everyone who'd bailed me out, I was still in the doghouse.

Matt shook his head mournfully. "We've had problems with the police before. The owners of the Pink Fish made a deal. We wouldn't let anyone sell outside our boundaries, and they wouldn't come inside looking. You just fucked all that up."

"Yea," I replied in a slightly too desperate manner. "But I paid them off. So …"

"No," snapped Jeff. "You just woke our Thai cop friend up that there was money over here again. What the fuck? He can come over next Friday and bust all our asses looking for more quick cash."

I slouched. Then listened to another verbal barrage of guilt-tripping. I was being cast out. And worse still, Anne was guilty by association. She gave me a hand palm whenever I tried to explain to her what happened. Just a simple joint at the wrong time. It's not like no one else was doing it. My only problem was some Thai cop was lurking around the bar and saw it. If I'd just stayed here and not bothered supporting her by going to the monastery, this would never have happened.

We were on the first boat out in the morning. Matt and Jeff had arranged a local taxi to drive us out to the train station, where we had two tickets to Bangkok pre-booked, along with an overnight sleeper train to Chiang Mai. Apparently, this was a good place to get far away from everyone and it had the added virtue of being filled with monks for Anne. Not that she was happy at finally going to a town full of monks and culture. She barely said a thing other than I had to pay for her tickets. Which I did. This led me to the additional problem of being nearly eight-hundred pounds poorer. It wouldn't have been so bad, except Anne had also thrown all my stuff out of our cottage. I slept outside all night on the porch. But the reality was I barely slept. Mosquitoes, sandflies, and the occasional meandering cockroach constantly kept me awake.

How quickly everything fell apart. How quickly everyone turned on me. How close an escape it had been with the police officer. Things could really have been worse for me. It seemed like I was the only one who saw this side of things. I felt bad everyone had to pay my fine, but I did pay everyone back. And I apologised. Yet, still. Here we are, cast out.

CHAPTER 10

THE DRAGON IN CHIANG MAI

Chiang Mai was our third major stopover in Thailand. The train trip had been brutal. Anne took the top bunk in a sleeper carriage and somehow I ended up with all our bags in the lower bunk. A thin blue curtain separated me from everyone walking by. All night. Worse yet, we were next to the internal carriage door, which did nothing but open and shut all night. Didn't people ever sleep on sleeper trains? Still, we'd arrived, and it seemed a little cooler at this end of Thailand.

Not only was there a cooler climate, but the old town was much more historic than either Ko Pha Ngan or Bangkok. Everywhere you looked, there were old walls, temples, and monks. Well, the monks were mainly behind the old walls and inside the temples, but they were there. I would have thought this would have helped Anne forget about having to leave our beach paradise. Instead, things were getting worse.

We'd arrived and checked into a small guesthouse in the old part of the city. Well, at least Anne checked in. I stood there like a moron as a door was slammed in my face. Apparently, she'd asked Matt and Jeff to make two separate room bookings. And 'only one' had come through. The guesthouse didn't have any other rooms either, other than one dingy dorm room. I took a bunk bed with the vague idea that Anne would somehow cool down and start talking to me again. Let me apologise for the hundredth time and then we could move on as a couple again. None of that happened, of course.

"I don't want you anywhere near me, Jonny."

"But Anne …"

"No," she snapped between the door crack. "You ruined this. You did. No one else. Just YOU!"

"What do you want me to do?" I pleaded. "I can only say sorry so many times. It was a stupid mistake. Could have happened to anyone."

"It didn't. It happened to you. And we all nearly got arrested because of YOU!"

A slight overreaction. Nobody got arrested. I lost eight hundred pounds and now we were in Chiang Mai. The perfect place for Anne to go Monk spotting.

"Yea, I screwed up. Can we move on? We're somewhere new. Can we at least look around?"

"I'm busy."

"Busy doing what?"

"Lunch."

"Okay, I can have lunch too."

"No, I'm busy."

"Oh, come on … Let's have lunch together and forget this."

"No. I'm having lunch with someone else."

"Who?"

Silence.

Maybe she'd lost the plot with all that dope she'd been smoking over the past few weeks. The door swung open and Anne stormed out. A heavy whiff of perfume trailed behind her.

"Where are you off to then?"

"Lunch."

"With who?"

Anne turned around with a spiteful look. "Stuart. I'm having lunch with Stuart!"

Fuck no. Not again. Not the know-it-all travel writer from a little of everywhere. I'd forgotten he had said that he was headed to Chiang Mai to do research or something. Worse yet, he was probably writing his memoirs. Then it hit me. How the hell did Anne arrange lunch with him when we only just arrived?

***

"Anne!" Stuart exclaimed. "Great to see you again."

Anne lunged into Stuart with a cheek to cheek kiss that lasted for far too long. Then, to top it off, she hugged him. Also, for far too long.

I was yet again the third man out and had to find my own chair to join them at the table.

"John," Stuart began slowly. "I hear you've been having some interesting times down south."

It was Jonny. Why was he being so formal? He immediately threw me off base.

"What? Who told you?"

Stuart ignored me and just nodded sympathetically at Anne. "Are there any other problems?"

Anne shook her head mournfully, "No, everything's fine. Just a bit tired after all the trauma of dealing with the police."

"Wait, wait." I continued, "How does everyone know about what happened?"

Stuart looked at me as if he knew everything, but was sworn to silence.

Anne finally cracked. "I emailed Stuart yesterday. Jeff wanted to know where to book our tickets to so I took a chance that Stuart was still here."

"And you told him everything?"

I was ignored again as a server came over and took our orders. Anne and Stuart were back in the whole let's talk about travel in Thailand zone again. With Stuart taking the lead guide role and Anne lapping it up like a cheerleader groupie. And if she wasn't flirting before, she was positively offering herself up when she mentioned having a single room.

I ate my Pad Thai noodles in silence, pretending to ignore the guide and flirt at the same table. Apparently, they were planning to visit some temples in the old city. Tempted as I was to go along and break up their merriment, I declined.

"You sure?" asked Stuart with excellent fake sympathy.

I nodded in defeat. The lack of sleep over the past few days had me thirsting for a lie-down. I should have asked about meeting up later. But I forgot. Instead, I pulled out my phone and wrote Charles a quick update via Messenger and to cover my ass just in case Anne let on what really happened.

> *In Chiang Mai now. Lots of crazy shit down south. Had to get out of Dodge literally. All is cool now, though. Catch you soon J*

Then there was an email to mum and dad.

I walked out into the tranquil street with the thought of going back to the guesthouse for some sleep. Then I remembered that I was in a packed dorm room. The idea didn't appeal. Taking to the streets of Chiang Mai, I noticed more dentists than massage parlours along the old streets. The city had a more family feel to it than Ko Pha Ngan or Bangkok. There was certainly no chance of a Haad Rin Beach Full Moon party here. Judging by the tourists around Chiang Mai, we'd ended up in a more middle-aged type of city. This must be their version of a Thai Island. Quiet, quaint, filled with restaurants, temples and altogether, not much to do.

I turned a corner on the way back to the guesthouse and a few girls wearing orange polo shirts stood up from a wooden bench. One with really red lipstick smiled at me and held out a brochure.

What was a two hand massage? Doesn't everyone have two hands?

I declined. Completely unsure about what I'd be letting myself in for after my Bangkok experience. The special four hand massage was simply beyond my current state of mind. I'd keep the idea in reserve for now. Didn't want to tip the boat any further. Going back to the guesthouse and getting some sleep seemed a safer option. I needed to get my head clear and work out how to fix everything. And if possible, try to get my own room.

I slept for a few hours in an empty dorm. Everyone else must have been out for the day. Finally, at around seven, I got up and walked to Anne's room. Empty, with the lights out. Dinner alone so. By nine, there was still no one in Anne's room. The receptionist eyed me like I was some kind of stalker. Fed up, I retreated back to the dorm room. I still couldn't think of anything to make this better.

At two am the first batch of Germans came thundering into my darkened dorm. Fluorescent lights on, they barked at each other for ten minutes before jumping into various squeaky iron bunks. A few more barks and then silence. The lights remained on.

At three am, two English types came in and turned the lights off and then on again once they realised they were on in the first place. The first must have kicked at least two backpacks and one bottle before collapsing into a lower bunk bed opposite mine. One loud fart later and there was silence.

"Engant Hoop Del Laada Ven!"

By four thirty, the Dutch had arrived. My eyes fluttered open briefly and stung under the harsh lights that were still on. No light switching on and off this time. Instead, it was a thirty-minute Dutch conversation with epic bass volume.

Just as I began nodding off, an alarm went off at five. The persistent beeping kind. This went on until finally one of the Germans pounded down from an upper bunk turned it off before rustling through a backpack that seemed to be filled entirely with plastic bags. It took them an hour to pack. Leaving just in time for the roosters outside to wake the barking dogs, who set off a string of loud Thai motorbikes.

***

"You look like shit."

"Thanks, Stuart."

Anne wasn't interested in my condition. It surprised me she even stuck around for breakfast. Though I was up before her, so maybe I just caught her before she snuck off for a day of Chiang Mai touring with Stuart. The good news in all this was that Stuart was leaving in a couple of days for Nepal or some other back of the book rated country. Music to my ears, and it was enough to get me through the day of listening to him talk about Chiang Mai's history. Anne loved every minute. Unsurprisingly.

"I'd love to volunteer and help the monks," she said, looking to Stuart for his opinion.

"Why?" I asked. "It's not like they're struggling or anything."

"They have nothing," Anne said, shaking her head. "Only the will to live a peaceful life with no possessions."

"Why volunteer then? I mean, if they don't want anything, then what help can you give them?"

I could see Anne's jaw tighten. Stuart came to her rescue.

"Many of the Monks around here live a simple life. But the world's changing. So things like teaching the young ones English can help educate them about these changes. Not a bad idea."

"See Jonny," retorted Anne. "not a bad idea."

I could have argued. But it seemed fruitless. Instead, I trailed along for the day as we visited Wat Jedee Luang and temple Chiang Mun, and back to another Wat Goo Come or something like that. By late afternoon, I was templed out. There are only so many enormous buildings with gold roofs you can take in a day. Even Anne seemed

81

to lose interest. Instead, she kept asking Stuart about Nepal and monks there. How I wish he'd just bugger off a day early.

My wish became partially true when he backed out of Anne's suggestion to have dinner together. Clearly, Stuart was not into Anne as much as she was into him. Thank goodness. Left with no alternative, Anne suggested that she and I have dinner alone in a local place. Finally, it seemed I was getting back into her good books!

***

"I'm leaving the day after tomorrow," Anne began as dinner arrived. "And I don't think you should come."

"What? Where are you going?"

She sipped a fruit shake casually. "I'm going to volunteer at a monastery?"

"Volunteer?! We should be making plans to go trekking in Northern Thailand. And then move into Laos or Cambodia. That was the plan … remember?"

"Plans change."

"We made the plans together."

"We're not together and things have changed."

"What? You mean the stupid thing in Ko Pha Ngan Island? Look, I told you …"

"I'm going to volunteer in Nepal."

"WHAT?!"

Fucking Stuart. She was going with Stuart to Nepal. All of a sudden, I felt the entire world shrink down around me. No wonder she'd asked for this one-on-one dinner. And no wonder Stuart had made excuses not to be there. I was being dumped!

"You're going with that twat, Stuart, aren't you?"

"He's not a twat," Anne snapped back. "You're just jealous."

"Jealous of what? The travel writer who's really just a would-be blogger?"

82

"See what I mean …"

"There's nothing in Nepal." That was a stupid thing to say, as I knew nothing about the place. But it was worth a shot as I figured Anne knew nothing about it either.

Anne shook her head and listed off things. "The Himalayas, Everest, rural life. The simple life. Buddhists. And it's cheap."

"So's Laos."

"I'm going to volunteer at an orphanage in Kathmandu."

This was clearly all Stuart's doing. He'd somehow got into Anne's head, with all her monk seeking ideas, and spawned the idea of getting her to volunteer there. After that, he could have his way with her. Which Anne was also, obviously, thinking too.

"How are you going to get there, anyway?" I said, trying to put up roadblocks on this whole insane idea.

"Stuart's arranging the tickets with Nepal Airlines in Bangkok. We're leaving here tomorrow. And flying on Monday."

There was a long, silent pause. I didn't even want to come to Thailand. I wanted Greece. Anne wanted the whole South-East Asia experience. Not me. And now she was dumping me in Thailand for Nepal, of all places.

'Look," she said, lifting her handbag onto the table. "Stuart said he can get you a ticket too."

Charming, I wasn't completely being dumped.

"But I don't think you'd like it there."

"Why not?"

"You barely like it here!"

"Do too."

Silence.

"How much is a ticket?"

"Five hundred dollars for a return flight."

"Shit, I can't afford that. I just had to cough up eight hundred pounds to bribe a cop and get up here!"

Silence.

"You do what you need to do. I'm going to Nepal to help orphans."

Madness. It was all madness.

After dinner, drinks were with the culprit in all this insanity, Stuart. I brought up the conversation about doing other things in Chiang Mai to make for a weak defence in staying put. Reading from my phone, it seemed there was actually a lot to do. But nothing that really appealed to me. Only Anne. It was worth a shot …

"How about visiting the Long Necks tomorrow?"

Stuart shook his head. "Some people say it's all a show. Made for profit by exploiting a tribe of locals."

"Visit the Tiger Kingdom?"

"Watching drugged up tigers being petted by tourists," retorted Stuart. "Not my idea of fun."

Anne nodded in agreement to all this.

"Trek into the mountains to a local peanut growing village?" I continued. Hoping Stuart couldn't find fault in that. "Lot's of cultural stuff here … Anne."

Silence.

"How long is the trek?" she said, looking over.

"Erm … five days. Five or more days … There's quite a few to choose from."

She looked over at Stuart for approval. He was busy checking his own phone. "Yea," he finally nodded. "If you choose a good trekking company, it can be a good way to see life in Northern Thailand. Sorry, I've just got to confirm my booking to Nepal. My visa runs out in a few days and I don't want to do another run to Cambodia to renew it."

"SHIT!" Anne began rummaging through her money belt to check her own passport's arrival stamp date. I felt all the blood drain out of my head and go hammering into my heart in a panic as I did the same.

"I completely forgot," she said, flicking open her passport.

"When did you arrive?" asked Stuart, as if he knew what the

problem was already.

"About a month ago," I answered, looking at the smudged blue stamp from Thai immigration.

"I think you get thirty days on arrival visa for here."

"Bollox," cursed Anne. "We've only got three days left!"

"We can extend," I added

"It's Thursday," said Stuart. "Tomorrow's a holiday and everything is closed until Tuesday. You'd best book a bus to Cambodia for Saturday."

"Cambodia?" replied Anne. "I wasn't planning …"

"Yes! Yes, we were." I added. "It's on our list."

"Or you can fly out to Nepal with me on Monday from Bangkok, like we'd planned."

"Yes!" Anne jumped up and hugged Stuart.

In the space of nearly twenty-four hours, my life had gone from living on a paradise island to being cast out to some third world country whose claim to fame was Mount Everest and the trots.

CHAPTER 11

ON TOP OF THE WORLD

"Namaste! Only one thousand rupees!"

"Ignore them, let's walk," shouted Stuart over the din of Nepali touts, all heaving towards us like it was the end of the world and we were the only ones that could save them.

Dozens of grubby faced short men all swarmed around us outside Kathmandu's international terminal. I'd never seen so many dirty, half-shaven faces in all my life. And why so short? And why were they all pushing against us? It was as if they were urging us with their bodies, in unison, towards their taxis. This was not a place to be claustrophobic. Or have issues with personal space. Which I have. Stuart led us through the masses of grimy, heaving men, all shouting that they had the best taxi price. They pushed us to the left, then to the right, and then, whenever there was any iota of space available, surged forward. If Thailand had touts, then Nepal was the spawning ground of the incoherent, rude, dirty, fallen from grace touts the world has ever known.

Once the touts saw Stuart knew where he was going, or more to the point, that he had no fear in shouting at them where he was going, they left the outer circle of our scrum. Reaching the other side of the car park, Stuart had somehow, by now, negotiated a fare with one man. We then squeezed into the smallest white Suzuki taxi I'd ever seen. Anne and I had just enough room in the back seat between the two of us and our daypacks. I didn't think it was possible to make car seats this small. Two bags went into the boot and the driver strapped one to the roof. Probably mine. Then we were off at speed in a car with no suspension and a driver with little regard for the mass of other vehicles around us.

During all this, I noticed Anne was smiling wildly while Stuart had a permanent grin as if he'd just arrived home after a long trip away. Our driver scowled in the rear-view mirror at me with blood-shot eyes. I avoided eye contact and looked out at the throng of people in the streets. Most dressed in the most deprived collection of clothes imaginable. Dark moustached faces occasionally glared back into our rear seat windows with these strange hung-over like red eyes that seemed normal in Nepal.

"Jesus, it's like the end of the world out there."

"Welcome to Kathmandu Jonny," said Stuart over our drivers near-constant car horn blasts. "There's nowhere else like it on earth!"

I couldn't imagine any other place on earth wanting to be like Kathmandu. The streets alone reminded me of rubbish dumps back home. I'd exchanged the land of a thousand smiles for a giant rubbish dump. To add emphasis to all this, our driver rolled down the window, letting in the smell of putrid burning plastic and rotting effluent. He then hacked up what seemed like an entire sinus and spat it out into the street with authority. I do not know if it hit someone. But if it did, then it probably felt like a right hook.

We turned up onto a narrow side street. The little Suzuki engine revved hard over potholes as we hurtled up a hill while avoiding the occasional motorbike, ancient bicycle, and of all things a stunned-looking cow coming in the opposite direction. Why was there a cow on the city streets? Nothing made sense. Now in a residential area, I could see that the rickety old red-bricked buildings here all had the same look as the rest of the city. Being on the verge of collapse. Naturally, this seemed like the place where we'd be staying.

We pulled up outside a guesthouse that looked a little more sturdy than the rest of the city. Unfortunately, it was sandwiched between two teetering buildings that seemed to slope inwards over ours. It really wasn't hard to imagine a strong wind sending everything crumbling down like Jenga blocks. Kathmandu's buildings were a disaster movie director's goldmine for a complete catastrophe on a budget.

"Namaste!!" shouted Stuart, swinging the car door open.

"Namaste!" replied voices in unison.

"Namaste!" Anne and Stuart replied in unison while pressing their hands together.

"Namaste!" said the little faces, looking at me.

"Nam … a … ste," I replied, completely unsure of what the hell was going on.

Namaste was the most popular word in Nepal, it seemed. It meant something like 'Peace be with you, hello and welcome' all rolled into one. Stuart's regular guesthouse was full of little people that liked to say it. Repeatedly. Whenever you walked into a room, they said it. Whenever you looked at someone new, they said it. Whenever you bumped into someone in the corridor, they said it. You wouldn't want to dislike saying Namaste in Nepal. Anne loved the word and repeated it to everyone that said it who then, naturally, repeated it back. It was like Groundhog Day the movie, but only involving one word. Meanwhile, as this was all going on, I still couldn't quite get past the fact I had exchanged pristine beaches and cocktails for terribly expensive beer and a city that looked like a war zone.

The one small bonus in all this is that I now had my own room. And it had an en-suite. All this for the same price as a dorm in Thailand. The downside was that the bathroom looked like something out of a pre-war public toilet. A cracked black plastic toilet seat sat askew on an enamel pan with yellow something growing along every edge. The decor matched the bedsheets. Yellowed with age and harbouring a strange mouldy smell. The only saving grace in all this was that Thailands overwhelming heat had been replaced by normal temperatures once again.

I threw down my bags and went back downstairs to meet up with Stuart and Anne for dinner. Apparently, we were going out to discover Dal Bhat. Nepal's traditional dish. I couldn't wait. But had to as Anne was taking a hot shower. Stuart said something about hot water only being available at random times during the day and night. Shanoli, the lady owner of our guesthouse, tried to explain it was to do with the power cuts and how stupid the system was. That was a bit rich coming from the actual owner! I tried to work out why you could only shower at random times as we eventually headed out for dinner. Evidently, there were power cuts every day in Nepal and so you had to plan your hot shower around them. Except if it was a hot sunny day when they didn't turn on the water heaters as they had solar power. Unfortunately, it wasn't electric solar but heated water solar, so it didn't always work well on cloudy days. Essentially, in Nepal, it seemed like a case of turning the tap on and hoping for hot water. Much the same as ordering from a Nepali menu for the first time.

"It's rice and lentils."

Staring at the large aluminium plate divided up into four sections, I looked up at Stuart. He ignored me. Instead, Anne took his attention by asking what all the little bits of goop were that ran out of their sections on the aluminium plate and into other sections. I was certain they weren't meant to do that, but due to the runny consistency or lack of proper preparation did just that.

"This one's curry. With cauliflower and green beans. It's really good."

"Hmmm," cooed Anne as she took a spoon of greeny coloured goop.

It didn't actually taste too bad. The rice was, well rice. And each little compartment of goop flavoured it all well. That is until you dipped your rice into the blood-red goop and ate the mix. Then your mouth burned like it was touched by bitter fire. As such, you instinctively gulp down the accompanying tea that tastes nothing like tea back home. It's more akin to some mix of lukewarm chocolate with tea stalks floating around in it.

"Watch out for the chilli Jonny."

"Thanks, Stuart. I got it."

Anne smirked as she saw my eyes watering, followed by my reaction to Nepali tea. I suddenly thought about what I had ever seen in her. The only reason I'd chosen to come to Nepal was because of her brother Charles. He'd have freaked out and come over himself if he'd learned I'd let her go alone. Or more to the point, go alone with Stuart. Things looked to be getting worse tomorrow as well. We were all off on a bus to some town called Pokhara. Stuart had suggested we take a short three-day hike to see the Himalayas before visiting some monk run orphanages for Anne to engross herself in. I saw nothing appealing about any of this apart from hopefully seeing Mount Everest. That would be cool.

We wrapped up dinner and took a walk through Thamel on our way back. Thamel was Nepal's number one tourist district, with a host of restaurants and guesthouses. It was also where at night bad eighties music blares out from various crumbling buildings where live local bands play. There were people and various forms of transport everywhere along the main single lane road. The people were the ones I was having serious problems with. There was no sense of personal space. Every single local seemed intent on shouldering me.

"You want smooooke?" I jumped back as some semi bearded man in a thick coat lunged, his dirty face so close to mine I could smell moist tobacco on his breath. "Hashishhhh? Smooooke?"

"No!"

"Smooooke?"

"Just ignore them," said Stuart, waving the dealer back. Anne ducked in close to him as the cacophony of human bombardment continued.

It got even more congested by a corner. There was no room to move out of anyone's way. Old men in rickshaws would trundle by, trying to snag your clothes on various bits of random metal that stuck out of their contraptions. While every thirty seconds or so, a motorbike would do the same. Only to be forced back across the road by one of the rampant white little taxis containing a demented driver in a waist coast constantly holding down the horn. There were no footpaths in sight, only random open drains with grey liquid and gaping deep potholes running alongside the storefronts. Moving closer to the storefronts to escape the homicidal traffic meant you then had to deal with various forms of human life trying to breathe their sales pitches into your face. A vision that was akin to something Dante could easily have written about. A horrible twisted nightmare that could only be God's sandbox to see what the end of the world would be like. I failed to think of something that could make this any worse.

"Monnnny, give me monnnney."

I jumped back again as some wild-haired boy no higher than my waist grabbed hold of my arm.

"No!" I yelped, pulling my arm back. But he held on. Tightly.

I became convinced he was in the process of mugging me. I was literally being accosted by an eight-year-old child, who, rather unsettlingly, seemed to possess the strength of a fully grown adult.

I tugged my arm away again just as a rickshaw trundled out and nearly ran me down before swerving wildly into the middle of the broken road with a clatter. I jumped into a doorway for shelter and to catch my breath, only to notice I was now surrounded by four more street boys all tugging at me like petty demons.

"Monnnney, Monnnney," they all chanted in dis-harmony.

Their faces were streaked in dirty black soot, and their clothes were thick with stiff grime. Each one was tugging at me with one hand while the other was either mouthing for food or holding a blackened palm open in front of my mouth. How on earth was this allowed in a 'tourist zone?' To cap it all off, I was still struggling with the fact I was essentially being mugged by a gang of small kids.

"GET OUTTA HERE!" roared Stuart.

I was shocked by his ferocity. And even more shocked that the children paid little heed. One looked at him with a scowl, while the others, at least, let go of my clothes. I took the opportunity and pulled away, past Stuart, and narrowly dodged a honking motorbike, which nearly forced me back towards the little hands. Another warning shout from Stuart and the street children chose not to follow as we finally continued back towards the guesthouse.

I stayed quiet on the walk. I couldn't understand why on earth anyone would choose to visit Nepal? It's a live version of a post-apocalyptic movie. The thought of what the buses were like for our five-hour journey to Pokhara had me seriously considering putting in a call to Charles and telling him his precious sister was on her own and I was going back to Thailand.

***

After nine hours, we were still on the bus to Pokhara. So much for it only being a five-hour bus trip. We'd been trapped for hours in the most desolate of towns called Mugling, due to road works. Both my butt cheeks were feeling physically bruised from the lack of seat padding. But being stuck due to roadwords wasn't the start of this journey. For at least three hours, we were stuck in traffic just trying to get out of Kathmandu. Well, actually, just outside Kathmandu. Or somewhere on the city border. Everyone had a different excuse, place name, and idea for the delay. It didn't quite make sense, like most things here. There was a strike on too. Apparently, there are at least two strikes every week in Nepal. The latest ones weren't just nationwide either. They were split up into regions. And when there's a strike, you're not allowed to drive anywhere unless you are on a tourist bus or have a specially coloured license plate. Even if you have nothing to do with the strike. In our case, moving out of Kathmandu city was fine, but in the next region, there was a strike. This meant there were three lanes of vehicles stuck in limbo-land on the official two lanes that were the only ones in or out of the capital city. No wonder the country was such a mess.

Being on a tourist bus, we were immune to strikes, so we were allowed to pass. Unfortunately, we were behind a very long queue of vehicles that were not allowed to pass. And so there was lots of honking of horns, engine turning off and men getting in and out of vehicles for no apparent reasons other than to spit or shout up the road at nobody in particular.

Spitting seemed to be Nepal's national pastime. Everyone spat. Men, women, children, even the monks on the bus spat. The older you were, the more right you had to spit on the floor than out a window. This was something Anne was not so enthralled by, as she had a window seat. In front of her was a monk who enjoyed scrapping his sinus out every twenty or so minutes. It wasn't just the internal sinus scraping sounds that he produced that made one's belly quiver; it was that he would gargle with the contents. Then, swish them to the left, then to the right of his mouth as if sampling a fine wine before inhaling and launching the repulsive contents out the window. With authority.

Stuart had had the sense to sit on the outside seat beside Ann, while I sat behind him with a skinny old Nepali man beside me near the window. Anytime I looked at the old man, he'd break out into a big toothless grin and sit up to attention. I tried saying hello but kept getting the repeated Namaste treatment. I replied with a Namaste once or twice and he'd nod before sitting back and releasing his smile into a placid look of neutrality. I'm guessing he wanted to ask me something but didn't know English.

During all this, I was also began suffering from an agony surrounding my stomach. I had the shits. Not bad, but not good. I went for most of the night at the hotel. I figured it must have been that retched dal bhat stuff we ate last night. Or that red goop that actually made my rectum burn as it exited. I took two Imodium and was now holding onto an ever-increasing bloated stomach. The actual discomfort came from a build-up of internal wind. I was terrified to release any gas in case anything else escaped, which was a high possibility as the bus bumped, lurched and bounced along the pothole ridden roads with reckless abandon.

"Should be there soon," said Stuart cheerfully chomping away on a sandwich he'd brought with him. "Keep a lookout on the right. You should see the Annapurna mountains soon."

By now, the old man beside me had given up grinning at me as I looked out the window. He sat there with a hand on his chin, staring out at the small concrete houses we drove by. During all this the driver honked the buses really annoying multi tune horn every time he passed anything with a pulse.

I wondered what the old man was thinking. Maybe why he was born into such a desolate country? Why were things so crap when you get old? Why the five-hour bus trip was now in its ninth hour? Did he find the toilets in Mugling as deprived as I did? Or maybe he was also thinking about a bloated gas build up from the food he had last night.

My stomach gurgled at that thought. I shifted my position to distract myself. Anne looked back. I could swear she was enjoying my predicament. How she survived all day eating nothing other than a packet of biscuits I didn't know. The monk in front of her gargled with his sinus contents again. I smiled, and she looked away.

"It won't take long to get to the guesthouse, will it?"

"No, it's right along Lakeside," replied Stuart. "We can walk if you want? Or take a taxi?"

"Taxi!" I said, knowing Anne might well choose to walk. "I could do with a toilet."

"You could have gone anytime we stopped," Anne rebutted.

"Have you seen the condition of the toilets out there?"

"Yes, I went in the restaurant we stopped at for lunch. Couldn't do it."

"It's a hole in the ground, Jonny," Anne said sarcastically. "It's Nepal. What do you expect?"

"A toilet seat?"

Silence.

What I didn't tell them is that I tried the squat toilet hole in the ground thing when we were held up in Mugling. I didn't have a choice. I tried twice. The first time, the wet concrete hole wasn't too bad. It smelled like a dark, dank alleyway with several cats living in it. The problem was I couldn't squat down far enough to relieve myself in it. Even if I was solid, I was still worried that something might rub against my trousers as it came out. How can you tell from that angle? But the main issue was I wasn't sure that what was coming out would be solid. Splashback on your pants while having to go out in public afterwards would not have been nice.

The more successful method was to remove my trousers and go for it, bottomless. Only the concrete cubicle had no place to hang anything. So, I retreated back to the bus and brought my day bag back to the toilet with me. The plan was simple. Remove trousers place them in my bag. Place bag on shoulder, squat and wait for a prompt bowel emptying. I even thought my luck was with me in one cubicle when I opened the door and saw a ceramic squat bowel. One step up from the concrete hole in the other cubicle. It even had little grips to place your feet. Then I saw the dirty little plastic bucket beside the bowl. It contained the water you were meant to clean yourself with. No toilet paper. Bare hands only. And then there was the constant sound of car, bus or truck horns outside. Was our bus leaving without me? And that's when I lost my nerve.

Not thirty-minutes out from leaving Mugling, after being stranded there for hours, and we stopped for a tea break! It was insane. I gathered together ragged tissues from various pockets in my bag and tried again in another concrete hole cubicle near where the bus was. I squatted down. But as I did, my bag slipped from my shoulder and touched the dark wet floor. Instinctively I used the tissues to wipe away the repulsive liquid. I knew my fate. Staring at the bum cleaning bucket again, I wondered how many other hands had been in there? How many other unwashed hands had scooped up the water? How many hands had just touched parts of their body covered in something you shouldn't touch, then dipped their hands into the bucket? My sphincter tightened to epic proportions, and I took two more Imodium. Next time I would not think about it. But I'd bring my own roll or two of tissue and maybe some disinfectant. If for anything, the smell of these places.

"You'll just have to adapt to Nepali ways, Jonny," continued Anne. "It's not England anymore."

"It's not Thailand either," I rebuked. "They had toilets. Good ones."

"Well, you took care of Thailand for us, didn't you?"

She would never let it go.

"There you go," interrupted Stuart, "Look out to your right."

Stuart had been right earlier. I'd never seen anything like it in person before. Set into a blue sky was a horizon lined with snow-capped mountain peaks. A surreal feeling took hold of me. Almost as if I was in a movie looking out at a cardboard cut out backdrop. Only this was very real. The bus driver blasted out more ear-piercing honks as more concrete dwellings flew past our window. Yet in the background of all this chaos was the most majestic mountain scene I could ever have imagined.

<h1 style="text-align:center">CHAPTER 12</h1>

<h1 style="text-align:center">CROSSROADS OF LIFE</h1>

Pokhara was instantly more likeable than Kathmandu. The main road, known as Lakeside, had virtually no traffic. There were even some cows wandering up and down looking for throwaways from the multitude of tiny restaurants and cafes that dotted the area. Although there were still people pleading for us to come in and buy something from their shops, they were a lot less aggressive than Kathmandu. But best of all, speakers that pointed out into the street playing various Buddhist chants often drowned them out. Yes, if there was an opposite to Kathmandu's congestive chaos, it was Pokhara.

Our guesthouse was an upgrade too. We each had our own rooms that were a little more upmarket than last night. Anne had made it public we would not be sharing a room any longer. There was no mention of our relationship. That was no longer even in the equation. The reason given for the new insistence on single rooms was that the prices for a single room here were now less than sharing the costs of a double in Thailand. I didn't have time to mount an argument. The truth was, I was just overjoyed at having a proper en-suite toilet for myself after nine hours on the bus. The only problem I was having with a toilet to myself was that nothing wanted to come out. My stomach ached like it really needed to go. And still gurgled whenever I thought about it too much. But even after sitting there for an hour, nothing happened. The extra two Imodium on the bus had completely sealed me up.

"We're leaving now Jonny!"

I opened the door to see Anne walking down the guesthouse corridor. Stuart was going to show us a place to eat before introducing us to a trekking guide friend of his that was to take us on a trek to see the mountains.

"I've not showered."

No reply.

Anne was getting to be impossible. The entire trip was turning into her private agenda, and I was being excluded. I really didn't want to go on a trek, either. What I wanted was a beach, an iced cocktail, a dip in the sea and some tasty food. Add in some great music to dance to at night and to get back on track with our relationship. Or maybe not after all this. For the first time since being with Anne, I was feeling like the entire relationship wasn't worth the effort. Yes, she was my first love, maybe, but I was now even questioning that. How could you love someone, and then start to dislike them so quickly? Maybe it never was love in the first place but infatuation. Was I that naïve? All I knew was that I didn't think I deserved to be left out like this.

Screw them. I took a lukewarm shower, changed into something clean and went downstairs in my own time. There was no sign of Anne or Stuart, of course. The receptionist didn't know where they'd gone, either. The only person that seemed to know was the old housekeeper lady who put her fingers to her mouth and pointed outside.

"They've gone to eat?"

The old lady smiled, and her face contoured into a map of deep lines. She nodded. My own face must have given away something sad. The old lady turned her head to the side as a puppy might. Her dark brown eyes glistened in sympathy as her smile widened again.

I didn't know what to do other than to say thanks.

Alone again, I walked out of the guesthouse and down the main road in hope of possibly spotting Anne and Stuart. It couldn't be that hard considering Lakeside really only comprised of one road and a few side streets. Passing shops, I was continuously greeted by Namaste's and invitations to go inside. I finally caved in on the greeting front and concluded the only thing to do was say Namaste back. The trick was to do it without looking at anyone. If you looked at someone who greeted you, and you greeted them and looked back at them, then you were in trouble. Before you'd know it, you'd be sitting in some shop being offered endless cups of weak tea with attempts at selling you the best and cheapest priced items in town.

Towards the end of Lakeside, the road continued on and down around a corner before turning into a dirt road. The shops also thinned out and you could get a full view of the lake they circled around. Sheltered by some green hills, the water was flat and quite tranquil. A few small paddle boats were bringing people from one side of the lake to the other. High above, on the opposite side, I could just about make out a white domed building. The World Peace Stupa, according to one of Stuart's many things to do around Pokhara if you wanted a hike. Briefly thinking it might be nice to visit it, I was reminded by my still bloated stomach that I'd not eaten all day. Maybe eating would help with the bowel purge I needed so desperately.

"Namaste!" A skinny man appeared from outside a small shop and waved at me as if we were long-lost friends.

"Namaste," I replied with a short wave, instantly forgetting my newfound rule. So naturally enough, before I knew what was happening, I was being seated at a small plastic table with a menu in my hand.

Dhal Bhat. Momos. Chikin Cuury. Buff Steaks. Fri Rice. Chikin Fri Papper Rice. Pizza.

The misspellings were horrendous, but the idea of eating a pizza appealed. I tried ordering, but the skinny man just wobbled his head from side to side when I asked for it. I wasn't sure if the wobble was a yes or a no. But considering he didn't move or write anything down, I guessed the wobble meant no.

Second choice, chicken fried rice. Again a wobble of the head. So I tried pronouncing it as they wrote it on the menu. "Ch i k in. Fri. Rice."

Another head wobble.

Resorting to elementary school tactics, I pointed to a picture of chicken fried rice on the menu. Again another head wobble, only this time the man countered me and moved his finger up to a picture of dal bhat.

I shook my head.

He wobbled his.

I'm now thinking the wobble means yes.

I pointed at everything else on the menu one by one and with each item, he'd point back to dal bhat and wobbled his head from side to side as if he didn't have any balance in his neck. I couldn't take it. I actually thought that he might be having some mental issues at this stage. I shook my head and stood up to leave.

Snatching the menu away from me, the man went from friendly to scowling at me as if I had just insulted his dignity. I bit my tongue and just shook it off. I was too tired after the bus journey to think about Nepali oddities. It could not possibly be a restaurant, with a menu and only one item on offer. Instead, I decided to head back to the main Lakeside area in the hope of finding somewhere better for an early dinner. It didn't take long before something came along offering a brief respite.

Spotting a street cart selling milkshakes, fruit juices and lassi's across the road, I opted for an attempt at getting some local vitamins plus some fibre encouragement for my aching bowels. A tall man who was wearing what appeared to be a towel wrapped around the top of his head manned the cart.

"Namaste."

"Namaste."

"What's a lassi?" I said, pointing to a named picture of what looked like a milkshake on the side of his rickety cart.

The man grinned at me, "Namaste! Lassie plain. Lassie banana. Lassie fruit."

"Namaste. I mean, what's a Lassi? What's in it?"

"Namaste. Plain Lassi?"

"No, fruit lassie. But what's in it?"

"Yes sir, fruit lassie."

It was pointless. I just nodded in defeat. The man began work emptying small bags of watermelon, apple, and banana into an old metal hand grinder type of blender. A line of rich fruit juice poured out the bottom and into a glass half-filled with thick white creamy liquid. He then covered it all up and shook the concoction with rigorous abandon. Even if it tasted bad, the show was worth the 20 pence it cost.

"Fruit Lassie," he said, dropping a straw into the now creamy, brightly coloured liquid and handing me the glass with pride.

I took a tentative sip. The slight, bitter tang and sweetness were instantly recognisable. It was a yoghurt drink. A lassie was the Nepali version of a fresh yoghurt drink. Just what the doctor ordered. I rounded up my brownie points and knew it would also make a good email to tell my mum about. With renewed confidence, I gulped it all down and spotted another vendor beside him selling popcorn and nuts. I was getting the hang of all this. Popcorn was full of fibre which might get me going again, so I bought a bag and munched away on the little white kernels on my way back into Lakeside proper.

My stomach was no longer gurgling by the time I got back to the centre of Lakeside from my brief excursion. The lassie must have done the trick, as my stomach was also feeling less bloated and sore. It only cramped up slightly when I spotted Anne and Stuart sitting under a restaurant canopy near the turnoff to our guesthouse.

"I must have missed you guys when I passed by a while ago."

"Really?" replied Anne nonchalantly. "I didn't see you."

"How's the stomach?" asked Stuart.

"Fine, fine. Better. So are you guys staying here or going back to the guesthouse?"

"We might go and visit Benji," replied Anne.

"Who's Benji?"

"He's a monk from Kathmandu. Our guide recommended that he come along with us on the trek."

"Guide? You mean the person we're going to meet to see if they're suitable to be our trekking guide."

Anne looked annoyed.

"Jeez Jonny, give it a rest. The guide is one of Stuart's friends here. He's taking Benji for free, out of respect. Benji works at an orphanage in Kathmandu and he's here only for a few days. We're just going to talk about the trek he's doing. That's all."

"Yea, never mind the monk. It sounds like you've already decided on a guide. And a trek?"

"So?"

"So? So, isn't it meant to be a group decision?"

"Stuart's guide is good and honest."

"Wait, since when is Stuart a part of our group?"

Stuart sat back in his chair as if to distance himself from the heated conversation.

Anne pushed her plate back and glared at me. "Stuart's going with us to Poon Hill," she quipped. "He's also the same person who helped us bailout of Thailand after you got us in trouble."

"We were not in trouble!" I snapped. "Our visas had nearly expired. Anyway, Stuart's only here because he wants to take photographs for his 'blog.'"

"Jeez, Jonny, you're so rude," Anne's face was getting red. "Stuart's helped us out more than you have. He sorted out our mess in Thailand because you nearly got arrested, which messed up our entire trip. And he's allowing us an opportunity to trek in Nepal. If anything, you should be saying thanks to him."

I clenched my jaw. This was all spiralling out of control faster than any of us wanted. An open street argument. And what looked like a forthcoming break up of the newly founded group? I just wanted the fighting to stop at this point. Clearly, I would never win.

"Fine," I relented. "Fine, we're a group. Okay. No problems." Anne glanced at me with suspicion as I continued. "We'll go as a group. But can you please drop the Thailand issue? It was a mistake. Okay? A mistake. We all make them."

"Whatever," mumbled Anne. "I just can't handle your constant moaning, Jonny."

"Moaning? Who's moaning?"

"You're like a little kid that needs to be looked after all the time. And then when you're left alone you mess up everything for everyone else."

"JESUS, Anne. I thought we just cleared the air. And now you're back at me again!"

"I just don't want to be on a trek and have you screw up again." She retorted snidely.

"Thanks, Anne. Thanks a lot. A great friend you are."

"Can't handle the truth, Jonny?"

"Oh, get lost, Anne."

I turned back down the road, fuming over Anne's snarky ways. It didn't help that Stuart was just sitting there as if he was innocent in all this. I grabbed some popcorn and vexed my anger with loud crunches. They would not beat me. I'd prove I was better at this travelling game than any of them expected. Turning back to them, I pointed down the road.

"Let me know when we're leaving on this trek. I'm off to buy a jacket for it." Then I paused and thought about how spiteful Anne could be. "And, try to give me at least twenty-four hours notice before we leave for wherever you decide!"

With that, I tossed some more popcorn into my mouth. Spat out an un-popped kernel and marched back to the guesthouse, still fuming. The game was on. I would not take any more crap from Anne. How dare she take over our holiday and invite someone else to join? And then, above all else, put more trust in that stranger over me. Let alone ridicule me in front of him. Actually, ridicule wasn't right. She just plain out insulted and mocked me in public.

I forced my hand into the little bag, pulled out a remaining handful of popcorn, and munched down on it. I'd show Anne what kind of man I was. I'd outdo them all on this trek!

C R A C K!!!

My eyes popped open in surprise, and my jaw dropped slightly. I didn't quite know what had happened at first. I thought I'd bitten down on another hardened kernel of popcorn. But something was amiss. There was a strange taste filling my mouth. My tongue moved over the ridge of my teeth, looking for the rogue kernel. Only as it did, it also dragged low over one tooth and felt a sharp edge.

Instinctively, I spat out the remaining popcorn. Something like grit was filling my mouth. I pushed a piece to the forefront and picked it out with my fingers. At first, all I could see were little white bits of popcorn mixed with darker bits of the slightly burnt kernel. But moving them between my fingers, I soon came across something white and hard. Then some more. Inside my mouth, I could feel more loose bits along the side of my jaw. Christ, I'd just broken a tooth!

CHAPTER 13

THIS WOULD NOT HAPPEN BACK HOME

The dentist's waiting room was only a cramped dark office with a row of dull wooden chairs lining one wall. There was barely enough space for one person to squeeze along the row to the end where the surgery door was. Thankfully, I was the only patient. If I wasn't so inebriated, I'd have cared more.

After a look in the mirror the previous night, I saw the horror of one of my rear molars cracked in two. The inner half was missing. All I could see was a rather ugly gaping hole in my white tooth and some ooze at the centre. The sensible thing would have been to locate Anne and Stuart to ask for his advice. But after the fallout, I couldn't bring myself to that level of despair. Instead, I moped back to the guesthouse and asked the owner, Mr Ram, if he knew of a good dentist. After he and his entire staff all took turns peering into my mouth and then recoiling in horror, they made some phone calls.

"It will kill any infection off," said Ram, pointing to a shelf full of local Khukuri rum. He wore a slim-fit blue striped shirt that constantly made me stare at his bulbous belly that even a mu mu would struggle to hide.

I wondered if he was the best person to call a dentist. His teeth were orange because of the strange nuts he ate. They frothed up in his mouth before he'd spit out a red liquid and carry on chewing. I refused the rum at least five times. I wanted a dentist and proper medication. But the entire process was a lot more complicated than it should have been.

"You must have bitten a stone in the popcorn," Ram concluded while constantly hitting redial on his landline phone. "Nothing else for it."

Everyone else agreed. The receptionist. The gardener. The old housekeeper lady. The boy who sits on one of the balconies and runs the moment he sees you. And the two families living next door who had also been invited round for a look.

I relented, took the advice, and bought a bottle of rum. Entrusting Ram to locate a dentist for me, I sat in a corner flicking my tongue over my missing tooth as if it would magically rebuild itself. The gardener and one of the male neighbours, both of whom spoke no English, took it upon themselves to act as my bereavement counsellors. They did all this for a glass or two of my rum while having an intense discussion about something in Nepali. It could have been the latest football match results, or it could have been about the stupid tourist beside them. I had no clue. So I just drank to stop them from finishing off my entire bottle.

It took an incredible two hours, but Ram finally made an appointment for early the next day. I tried explaining the emergency of the situation but all I got in return were head wobbles. When they got bored with that, they all left. But not before a final shot of painkilling Khukuri rum each.

The next morning, I was informed that the dentist had allegedly been called away on an emergency. The irony escaped everyone except me. Ram gave me some dal bhat for breakfast while I waited. Surprisingly, my tooth didn't hurt. It just felt cold. So, I thought it was best to eat something. The dal bhat had thick chunks of some sort of gristly meat in it. I was informed the meat was in fact goatskin. I shuddered at the thought.

Despite my stomachs gurgling, I was still constipated, but that thought of goatskin definitely loosened soothing in my colon. The owner had just the solution and offered me another bottle of rum with a big smile. I drank half a glass just to wash away the rubbery goat skin taste. I couldn't eat any more. The rum was quite filling. This continued on a bit until I realised I was being bundled into a taxi by the guesthouse staff with directions shouted at the driver repeatedly. I certainly did not know where we were going. And that is the story of how I was more than a little tipsy and got to the dentist's office.

A door in the waiting room opened and a girl who was thirty minutes ago the receptionist came out wearing a green facemask and nurse's uniform.

"Mr Jonny, the Doctor is ready for your surgery now."

Surgery? I wasn't quite sure what she meant. I just wanted to know how bad it was. Well, I knew it was bad. The gaping hole made that bit obvious. The truth was, I didn't have a clue what to do. I'd never had a tooth just crack in half like that. At best, I just wanted a little filling to tide me over until I got home.

I followed the nurse into the 'surgery'. There were two old wooden chairs by a small square window on the far side. A few dark shelves with scatterings of dental paraphernalia ran along pale blue walls. The terrifying highlight of the room stood at the centre. An ancient black iron dentist's chair that looked very ominous and very torturous in a medieval way. A Nepali man in a white coat and green face mask was busy laying out some silver instruments alongside the torture chair.

"Please be sitting Mr Jonny."

I followed the nurse to the iron chair and sat in its creaking metal frame. The thin brown padding that made up the seat was still intact, but all the same, I wondered if the whole thing wouldn't collapse at any moment.

"So then, Mr Jonny," said the Dentist. "Is it a tooth problem then?"

This was not a good start.

The dentist loomed up in front of me as the iron chair suddenly started reclining back as the nurse slash receptionist pumped away with her leg on some crank mechanism under me.

"Yea I ..."

There was no time to say anything. Before I knew it, the dentist had a long silver dental tool in my mouth. He let loose an immediate 'Ahh!' followed by some head waggling and a couple of frowns.

After about thirty seconds, the Dentist confirmed that I had cracked my tooth. And it had splinters. I had no idea a tooth could have splinters. I then realised that we were probably having some 'lost in translation' problems. So I just nodded and let out the odd confirmation grunt, as if I knew exactly what he was on about. He dived in again with a little circular mirror. My head began spinning from the alcohol breakfast and I was starting to feel nauseous.

Sitting back, he proposed a root canal and or crown. I never asked how much it would cost or which one I needed. I didn't have much of a choice either. A super-thin needle appeared and was promptly inserted into my mouth as if it was all pre-planned.

"Let me know if you are feeling this," he blurted, quickly.

How? My mouth was wide open, and I was terrified to even swallow. I feel a little prick. Then a cold sensation. Then nothing. Another prick.

Pain!

I grunted.

We quickly developed a system where, if I grunted, he stopped most of the time. Then, after two seconds, he'd start again with more shots of whatever he was putting in my gums. The more needle pricks I had, the colder my mouth became. Soon I felt nothing.

The nurse tugged at my arm and I realised I had been gripping onto the side of the iron chair so tightly that my fingers had gone white.

"Please rinse Mr Jonny," she said without a hint of sympathy.

There was blood. Huge globs of red puss plopped out of my mouth into the metal basin I spat into. Followed by some little white bits that made a tinkling sound.

The nurse pushed my shoulder with the strength of an ox, and I forcibly rested back in the chair. On the other side, I saw the dentist adjusting a large hook-like utensil and then a long thin instrument that resembled pliers. My hand instinctively reached out for the iron chair's side again. Only this time, it was met with the soft, warm touch of a human hand. It was soothing at first. Then she squeezed it hard as the dentist approached. This is when I retaliated with my own squeeze back. All I could think of was that I might end up breaking her hand.

The dentist's long pliers entered my mouth like a 747. I felt my heart rate rise at the dread of the incoming agony that was about to hit me. I tried desperately not to squeeze the nurse's hand, but it had no effect. I couldn't budge her fingers. Her grip was harder than the metal chair.

There was some tugging, and I felt bits break off from my tooth. There was no pain. Only the sensation that stuff was moving in my mouth where it shouldn't be. Another tug and something wobbled before a larger chunk broke off. More long needles. Some not so clean rubber dental gloves moved closer into my mouth. The dentist pushed down onto my tooth and I yelped instinctively. The nurse's hand began a crushing squeeze, and I wondered if I heard my knuckles crack.

More needles went back, and I was told not to swallow, which of course made me want to. Then the worst of the worst appeared. The drill. It entered my mouth and spun up in a high pitch. My jaw vibrated under the heavy drilling pressure and I could swear something poured out of my tooth. The nurse placed a suction instrument into my mouth and a loud gargled sound filled my ears as liquidised bits of my mouth were sucked away.

An angle pick went in next and the Dentist pulled at what was left of my tooth with it. During this, something chipped away and flew out of my mouth up onto my face, causing me to blink. Then another. He couldn't have done more damage with a hammer and chisel.

The dentist said something I couldn't make out with his mask on. I panicked a little in case he needed a reply. I did not know what to say. He fetched something else from his tray of instruments. What else did this man need to do to convince me I no longer needed a tooth? A clipper appeared and then disappeared under my eyes. I felt something clink against my other teeth. Then the dentist put a thumb on my cheekbone and I could see his face wince up in effort. Something's going on and I couldn't quite work out what it was? Was he pulling it out?

S N A P!!!

My eyes popped open wide, and I looked around, wondering what had just broken. The dentist's shoulders relaxed back, and he pulled the clipper out of my mouth. Apparently, he had to cut away a piece of the tooth before he was able to fill it. I was shaking and cold. I should have just flown home instead of realising the treatment I'd be getting here.

There was a brief time out as the dentist made up some sort of paste that would presumably be a part of my new tooth. The nurse also took the opportunity to take back her hand. It had white marks where I'd squeezed the blood out of it. I tried to smile, but as I did, some damn awful red glob of puss oozed out of my mouth and fell onto my chest. She offered a bib. As in an actual baby's bib and stuck it around my neck. I collapsed back in defeat. Despite not being in actual physical pain, all the pulling, pushing and snapping had me feeling like they had beaten me up badly.

Another instrument appeared, and this time it bore the menace of a metal file. The dentist bore down on the remains of my tooth and ground it into some sort of dental foundation. Then, taking the paste he'd created, he filled it all up into some sort of sculpture in my mouth. Another thirty minutes passed, and it was over. There was no mention of a root canal, crown, or even a mirror to see what had been done. I just paid two thousand rupees, about fifteen quid, and was told to be on my way.

I don't know how I got back to the guesthouse. I remembered swallowing a few painkillers the dentist gave me. A little man in a little white car shouting at me about no change outside the front door of the guesthouse. I also remember the indignation at seeing Anne and a monk sitting in the main lobby area when I got back.

"What happened to you?"

I knew why they were there. My stomach let loose a very loud nervous gurgle.

"Bwoke, ma toofth," I said through a mouth full of cotton swabs and stitches.

"Really?"

I nodded.

Anne looked at the shaven-headed monk in orange robes and then back at me. I was half hoping for just an ounce of sympathy. But was beginning to know better.

"Well … we're heading off tomorrow," she said, pulling out a small trekking map. "Just wanted to let you know."

I raised my eyebrows in submission.

"So …" started Anne. "Will you be coming?"

I figured every time I opened my mouth I was pulling at the stitches that I could just about feel were still under the aesthetics protection. The dentist had said I'd be okay for another few hours. But warned that I needed the painkillers he was giving me plus antibiotics and anti-blood coagulant to avoid any 'undue discomfort'.

"No, uohh go onnn," I replied, trying not to gargle out any blood. "It fine, uohh go. Vye."

I could swear Anne was beaming like a school kid getting their way behind the solemn nod she gave me.

"Can I leave my stuff in your room when I'm gone?"

The cheek of her to ask. I just nodded, waved them goodbye and climbed up the stairs. To hell with Anne. Let her go trekking. She was with a monk and Stuart. She'd be fine. The dull ache of the anaesthetic wearing off was now preoccupying my mind along with my stomach, which seemed to be also aching, again.

CHAPTER 14

FLUSH

The only thing worse than being left alone with the remains of a bloody stump of a tooth as the anaesthetic wears off is when the Imodium wears off at the same time. Instead of spending the evening in bed with painkillers, I spent it sitting on the toilet listening to my stomach empty out at least two days' worth of buildup.

With each purge, I swayed awake on the bowl. I wasn't just expelling diarrhoea. I had a full-on gushing waterfall under me. With each gush, a torrent ripped into the toilet bowl like a power hose. Between the hours of nine and eleven, this torrent seemed to trigger the pressure on my tooth, which then throbbed like a demented cohort of mockery.

Every thirty minutes I'd feel the blood fill up the cotton swabs in my mouth and I'd have to spit them out. And as the aesthetic completely wore off, each time I spat out a mass of red cotton wool, it felt like a part of my gum was coming out too. Not two seconds after spitting this out and, it was back to the toilet bowl for another power hose purging. I'd heard of both ends going, but this was a whole new game. Adding to all this, were Anne and Benji the monk showing up briefly to dump her bags in my room before scampering off. Perhaps the noise of me in the loo had something to do with it.

By two in the morning, I was a mess. My stomach growled anytime I swallowed my blood. So I spat every dribble out instead of swallowing. I took more painkillers and waited. I took the anticoagulants and waited. I took the antibiotics and waited. Finally, by three in the morning, the anticoagulants seemed to kick in and the blood in my mouth was clotting up. Now, instead of bright red cotton buds, I spat out dark brown swabs of semi-coagulated blood. Then it was over to the toilet, sitting down, shivering, and listening to the gush under me. Each time wondering about how much water my body holds? By four, my rectum was clenching and throbbing out nothing but a sphincters pout. That was my answer to how much liquid I had inside me.

Miserable, I fell asleep thinking of my precious island, clear seas, and, for some reason, a massage table in Bangkok. Memories of the Thai masseuse, the bar, the island, and the bikini girls around the campfire swirled around my head as I lost focus.

"N A M A S T E!"

It was the third or fourth time that hour I heard the now raised woman's voice in between the constant knocking. It took thirty minutes just to register it was my door that was being knocked on. And then another five to muster up the anger to throw back the sheets and storm over to throttle whoever it was. Only when I tried to stand up, my head spun and my tooth reminded me how feeble I was. The mere act of sitting up seemed to place enough pressure on it to make me think it was about to erupt like a volcano. I slowly wrapped a sheet around myself and staggered to the door.

"Namaste!" grinned a wrinkled face. I just about recognised her.

It was the old housekeeper lady.

Why was she there? Surely to god she didn't want to clean my room this morning. She looked at me and grinned again. Then she leant over to the side and picked up a tray. I looked down at a bowl of white stuff with red seeds on top and a little glass of orange juice. Breakfast? The old lady had brought me breakfast. I looked at her and tried to smile. But when I did, my stitches wrenched, and I grimaced. Spluttered. Coughed. And yelped in a very pathetic manner.

The old lady's face never changed from her big smile. She looked down at the tray, then back up at me. Then she pushed it into my hands and waved me off. Charming.

I wondered if the juice would be a good idea. Vitamin C was good for healing things. Then I remembered I could barely open my mouth without my stitches causing me to whimper. That's when I noticed the straw beside the glass. The old lady was thoughtful enough to give me a straw. I felt a longing for home.

I closed the door and shuffled over to the bed. I sat down and wondered why I deserved all this? Thoughts of Anne, Stuart and Benji the monk on the way to the mountains, filled my mind. They were happy. My life sucked. It really sucked.

"Namaste!"

The old lady was knocking at the door again. Could I have no peace in this country? I shuffled back over just as she began knocking again. How could I explain to her I didn't want anything other than a time machine to fast forward my life until I was in England again?

The housekeeper lady was still grinning. I could swear the lines around her old face made her look permanently happy. She held up a small flask of brown liquid. Then pretended to take a sip and slosh it around her mouth.

"K u k a r i," she said, nodding and placing the bottle in my hand.

I read the label and remembered my pre-dental medicinal efforts.

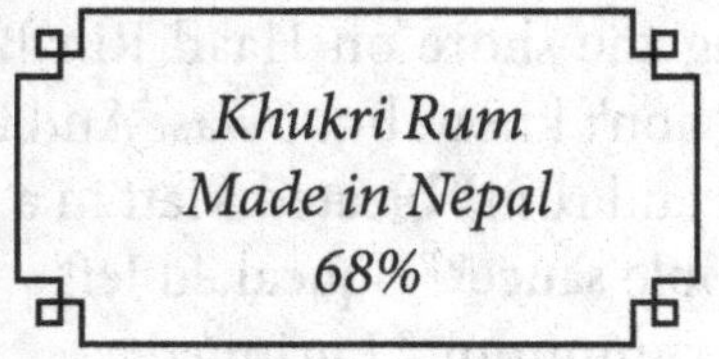

The old dear was giving me some old school medicine. I gave her a thumbs-up sign and tried to shake her hand. But as I did, she grabbed my wrist, came close, and placed something in my hand. She nodded vigorously, laughed, and turned to leave.

I looked down and opened my fist. She'd given me a small striped cloth bag. It was light, but there was definitely something inside it. I pulled open the drawstring and peered in. A small packet of rolling papers peeked back. Closing the door, I emptied out the rest of the little bag onto my desk. Rolling papers. Some tobacco. A matchbox and some scrunched up newspaper. I opened up the newspaper and out fell something resembling a chunk of dark brown earth.

Never.

My first smoke of hashish went straight to my head. I fought back a grin. Staggered over to the bed, took some more painkillers and fell into a dreamy state. My mind took me back to the island … back into the sea … I finally relaxed into a deep sleep.

***

My first cocktail of painkillers, antibiotics, Nepali hashish, and rum had me lost in another realm for the first few days. The truth of the matter was that I only recall taking the painkillers once. The old lady's 'tobacco' seemed like the best medicine I'd ever had or needed. Not that I knew where the hell I was half the time. Some rum for during the middle of the night, a smoke, and I was back asleep and in a far better place.

Splash, splash!

It was Matt and Jeff in their pink t-shirts bringing me cocktails while I floated along the shore on Haad Rin Beach. How I could float along a shore I don't know, but I was. And it was cool.

"Dude, Red Bull and rum," bleated Matt in a high-pitched voice.

"Red Bull and apple sauce?" Squeaked Jeff.

"Kuuuukar eee rummmm!" I grinned.

I drank and rested back in the floater along the shore, watching the clouds spin into little white cotton wool animal shapes. A lion merged into an elephant, into a duck. And further along, a whale became a map of Russia that morphed into a big raindrop.

Water splashed over me.

I turn over to see the girl from the Bangkok massage parlour splashing me with water. She was so beautiful.

"Massssaaaage?" she coos. "You want massssaaaage?"

"Yes. Yes. Yes!"

I couldn't remember the word for please in Thai. So I made one up. She seemed to understand. I turned over and felt her soft hands on my back. Each finger worked away streams of tension. I drank from a straw in my glass and felt the rum soothe my mouth. Then I started to eat some steak. I have no idea why the girl wanted me to eat steak, but it was there.

I chewed and chewed, but it was quite tough. I wondered how to tell her she was great at a massage but terrible at cooking steak. I worked the meat around my mouth, but no matter what, it refused to break up. So I leant over the floater and secretly spat out the steak. It hit the water with a plop. I watched as it floated down into the sea. Little coloured fish appeared and pecked at it. So many little fish. They swarmed around the meat and pulled at it until it all broke away. And still, they came. The floater started to bobble and sway as the fish kicked up into a feeding frenzy. I turned over.

"Opps, gotta move the fish are … Jesus! Anne!"

Anne was there, staring down at me. Her face flushed and her body was naked. She pulled an orange robe on.

"Jonny, you twat! Look what you've done. You killed the fish."

I sat up and looked around. The water was filled with dead fish. My steak must have poisoned them all.

Anne stood back and shook her head, "You killed them all, Jonny!"

Behind her Benji the monk appeared, "Bad things happen to bad people."

"I … I didn't do anything?!"

"Yes, you did!" denounced Anne. "Look at your teeth! They are rotten with guilt. It's all your fault."

I reached up to my mouth and felt my front tooth. It was loose. I waggled at it and with ease, it started to come out! Panic overcame me, so I did my best to push it back in. It popped gently back into its slot with a snap. But then I felt another come loose. So I pushed that one back too.

"Mr Jonny, I help!" It was the dentist. My mouth opened as his head disappeared inside.

"Don't bite down Jonny!" Mr Prapawat, the Thai policeman, was there staring at me. One hand on his gun. "I shoot you if you bite his head off."

"I put them back fast," said the dentist, reappearing from my mouth and brandishing a rubber mallet.

"No, I can do it myself," I said, grabbing the rubber mallet.

I then began knocking my teeth back into place by tapping them into their loose sockets. If you've ever seen the game where you've got to hit a mole on the head as it pops out of a hole, then you get the sort of frantic rate at which my teeth kept becoming loose.

"Don't mess this up, Jonny," taunted Anne.

"Mista, you wanted special maaaasssaaaage?" asked the Thai girl.

"The fish, the thousand fish you ended them," condoned Benji, the monk.

And so they all kept repeating the same thing over and over again as I desperately tried to knock my teeth back in with the rubber mallet. I sensed my breathing becoming more panicked with each thrust of the mallet. I frantically felt for more loose teeth, but with all the effort my floater began bobbing up and down uncontrollably.

"Don't fall over, Mr Jonny," shouted Mr Ram, the guesthouse owner.

"It's all over Jonny," Anne said, shaking her head. "You killed the fish. And it's coming for you!"

"Whap?" I couldn't talk with the hammer in my mouth.

The waves got bigger as Anne looked at the horizon behind me and laughed. I turned around and saw a giant blue whale powering towards me above the waves. It looked angry. Its big eyes looking at all the baby fish I'd killed. It got closer and its mouth opened. A giant black abyss.

I tried to paddle backwards, but the dead fish jammed my floater in behind bits of steak that now lined the shore. Everyone was gone, but I could hear them in the distance. Laughing. Taunting. Saying I was getting what I deserved. The whale's large tail splashed down, and it closed in on me. So close I couldn't see behind it anymore. All I could see was the huge black gaping hole in its mouth. Water poured in as it rushed closer towards me. Closer and closer until I began to tip into its gaping jaws and fall into its dark, conclusive mouth.

"NAWWWWWOOOO!"

I sat up in a frenzied panic and beat back at the air.

Panting as if I'd just run a race, I looked around through sleep encrusted eyes. I was in the guesthouse room. My body was wet from sweat. Beside me on the pillow lay two well-chewed dark brown blood-soaked cotton swabs from my mouth. Under them lay a large pool of my dried-up bloody saliva from where I'd been drooling.

I began to recall the bad trip. The steak, the dead fish, my teeth. I reached up to my teeth. Still there. Still good. Not lose. Pushing the foul pillow back, I lay back down. I might just have ignited a part of my mind I never, ever wanted to see again.

CHAPTER 15

FINALLY ...

I stayed in my room for a total of four days; I think. Things were certainly a little groggy. What I recall with regularity was the old housekeeper lady coming around every morning with a tray containing a bowl of yoghurt with fruit, juice, a straw and a small matchbox hidden under some paper napkins. Inside the box was always a nugget of hashish. I'd grown an aversion to it, though. The mixing of this plus painkillers and antibiotics had me in fear of going back into an intense hallucination trip again. I saw the danger.

Everything that had happened over the past couple of weeks had left me questioning my mind, life, and mental reasoning for being here. While my tooth looked to be healing, my mind was falling apart. For the first time in my life, I was feeling depressed. Not just exam or broken-hearted depression. I actually felt like I'd stepped down into a dark place that didn't want to let me out. I wanted to go home. I should never have come to Nepal. In fact, I should never have gone on holiday with Anne in the first place. That was the crux of all this.

Despite this feeling, the old housekeeper lady had been the light I needed every morning to pull myself out of bed. I placed some money on my empty tray every evening for her. I'm sure it was costing her to provide my natural cure-all. And I still didn't

120

understand why she was doing it. She didn't wait around to tell me, either. Sometimes I never opened the door until well past midday. But today I made an effort to listen out for her and get there in time. If for anything, to say thank you.

I heard the tap of a wooden tray on the floor. When I opened the door, I only glimpsed her shadow as she disappeared around the corner.

"Namaste!" I croaked.

"Namaste," said a voice from beside me.

I jumped back in shock.

"Jesus mate, are you alright?" said the voice in equal shock. A young Nepali guy with an English accent was coming out of his room beside mine.

"Erm … yea," I croaked again. "Broke a tooth. Had it repaired."

The guy walked over, but kept his distance a little. While he certainly looked Nepali, he was dressed in distinctly western garb. A pressed yellow shirt with an open collar. Faded designer jeans and some expensive-looking designer sandals. "Shit, that sounds bad. How is it?"

"I dunno," I replied truthfully. I'd only checked once to see if was still there. My tongue instinctively swiped around my mouth. Yep, it was still there. And aside from the wiry bits of stitches in my gum, everything felt fairly normal. "Umm, I guess it's not too bad." I finally nodded.

"You on some sort of meds for it then?"

I nodded again. "Too many I think."

The guy laughed and came a little closer. "Yea mate, you look pretty wasted, to be honest."

"I guess so. Wasn't really expecting a broken tooth here."

"Yea, I can imagine. Look, I'm off out to find some better internet. Do you need anything? Like, maybe some food or something?"

I'd been pouring the old ladies' bowls of yoghurt down the toilet. No idea why. I got into some notion it would infect my tooth. The thought of food suddenly made my stomach rumble. I then looked down and saw my dirty stained t-shirt smeared with dried blood, white yoghurt, I think, goop and patches of something else. My feet were also hideously dirty, for some reason. I must have looked an utter mess.

"Yea, actually some food wouldn't be a bad idea, I guess," I said. "Not sure what I can eat with this tooth though."

"Bananas and curd?"

"Curd?"

"Yea, it's like yoghurt. Only they call it curd here. It's actually superb when you're sick. Easy to swallow, no chewing and all that."

I nodded again. "Sounds good. Let me get you some money."

"No, it's alright, later. When I bring it back."

"Cheers, I appreciate it. By the way, what's your name?"

"Viktor," said the guy. Then, with his right hand, he wrote in the air. "Viktor with a K."

"Jonny," I said, holding out my hand.

Viktor looked at it and raised a finger. "No worries mate, later for the introductions and all that. Maybe you should have a shower or something now you're feeling better."

I looked at my outstretched hand and could see why no one would want to shake it. Pale. It was streaked with more dried blood and smudges that I couldn't identify. I nodded in agreement.

"By the way, where are you from?" I asked, as Viktor locked his door and headed off.

"London, born and bred," he replied. "Catch you soon. Enjoy your wash. I think there's still hot water."

Viktor was English? I wondered if I was still not 'with it' as I went back inside my room. All the same, he was right. I stripped myself down and stood back against the steaming hot water in the shower. A week's worth of grime, dried blood, and what I finally discovered to be spilt yoghurt ran off my body. Looking in the mirror, I wiped away the condensation and stared in horror at the person in front of me.

A pale face with bright blue eyes that had lost their sparkle stared back at me. Blackish circles under my eyes ran down into sharp cheekbones and sunken cheeks that were covered in a wiry beard. I'd never grown a full beard so fast in my life before. It all looked strange. Like a mini Robinson Crusoe on a desert island with no sun or food. The reality was I looked more like some homeless hobo type that had lost the will to live. Depression washed over me again. It triggered images from the bad trip to bounce around my mind.

Slumping back into bed, I pushed the dirty, bloodied pillow as far away as possible. The bed sheets were grey and equally dirty, which didn't help me feel any better. I'd gone from a carefree guy out of university with a girlfriend to a lonely broken down hobo in a dirty hotel room at the end of the world who was plagued by guilt. Guilt for making a mistake in Thailand and being told I'd messed up everything for everyone. Guilt for thinking I'd fallen in love with a girl that everyone had said was great and then stupid enough to tell her that. Rejected by all, I pulled the grimy bedsheet over my head. I deserved the grime. It fitted me for once. Where had it all gone wrong? I was so stupid. A few hours passed and just as I was about to fall back to sleep, there was a knock on my door and an English voice called out my name. Viktor.

"You still look like shit, mate," he said, handing me a bag full of bananas. A tub of what he said was chilled curd, and a big bottle of water. "And your room needs some serious fumigation."

I knew he was right. I felt another wave of guilt come over me.

"Yea, it's just me here so I haven't really … Anyway, how much do I owe you?"

"One-fifty should cover it," Viktor replied as he gingerly entered my room. "Bought them at the Pokhara supermarket in lakeside so it's a bit of a rip-off."

I handed him two hundred rupees and told him to keep the change. It was only something like fifty pence, but I didn't think it proper to ask for money back from a stranger who'd just helped me.

"No worries," said Viktor, pocketing the money. "So you broke the tooth out trekking or what?"

"No, I broke it here. Not been trekking … well, I couldn't go, actually."

"What? Because of your tooth?" Viktor had a quizzical look on his face. A rather strikingly handsome face that went well with his smart attire. He certainly wasn't a backpacker.

"Yea," I replied with a defeated shrug as I placed the tub of curd on the table in my room next to my laptop.

"But it's better now, right?" asked Viktor, as if the world was so easy. "Well, it will be better in a day or so, yea? So you can still go?"

My heart sank a little. "No, not really. We … I was meant to go with some others but they left."

"What? Left without you?"

I nodded.

"Are you guys stuck for time or something?"

"No, just arrived. I think we've got about six weeks left before going home."

"Seriously," said Viktor, opening his eyes up a little. "If you don't mind me asking like, but who did you come over with? I mean, if you have all that time, couldn't they have waited for you to get better? Or even look after you instead of leaving you here all alone?"

I have no idea whether it was how Viktor said it. Or how he ran through the list of reasons why they'd left me here. Or how a complete stranger just wrapped up everything that was depressing me in under twenty seconds, but it pulled at my gut and made my eyes sting. Before I knew it, I was starting to cry. Worse yet, it was in front of a complete stranger.

"Whoa, steady on, mate," said Viktor, looking a bit horrified at the emotional mess of a guesthouse neighbour he'd just helped out. "I didn't mean to like, upset you or anything."

I held my hand up and wiped away a wet patch under my cheeks.

Shit, I was a mess. I'd not cried since I left home for university. And even then, it was only when my mum started bawling in the driveway as my dad drove me off.

"Sorry, I … I don't know what's wrong. It's just. It's just a fucking mess."

With that, I breathed deeply, sucked back the sadness and let loose the whole story about Anne in under a minute. Our brief secret relationship, signing up for the discount student holiday together, the breakup, reunion in Thailand, the near arrest in Thailand and how we ended up in Nepal. And, how I really, really hated Nepal.

I could summarise my last year in under a minute. Was that all it was worth? I felt my heart drop again.

"Shit mate, sounds like you've had a bad time alright." Mused Viktor.

Again, I just nodded.

"And she just fucked off with this Stuart and the Monk?" recoiled Viktor. "Even after seeing you with a broken tooth?"

I kept nodding and then blew my nose on some tissue paper. "She's probably shagging him right now."

"Shagging who? The monk?!"

"No. Stuart. She's had the hots for him since Bangkok."

"Fuck me. Sounds like she's done a number on you alright."

"Thanks, mate."

"Yer, no worries."

"No, I mean thanks for reminding me she's probably doing some guy right now in the mountains."

"Oh," frowned Viktor. "Well, if it's any consolation, having a shag when trekking in the mountains isn't such a great thing."

"Huh?"

"Yea, mate, the room walls are all paper-thin up there. You're all sweaty from trekking and probably haven't had a good wash in a while either. A pretty grimy shag if you ask me."

I shrugged. This didn't make me feel any better.

"Anyway, what trek are they on?"

"Poon Hill or something."

"That's not far. She'll be back after a week or so I guess."

"What? You've been on that trek?"

"Yea, I did the whole Annapurna circuit about a week ago. Took nearly three weeks."

"Sounds impressive."

"No mate," laughed Viktor in what I deciphered was a slightly posh cockney accent sneaking out. "I hated every bloody day of it."

"Why? What happened?"

"Long story," replied Viktor, shaking his head. "But let me put it to you this way. Long days. Dust, wind, the same crap food every day, and a lack of showers had something to do with it."

"Oh, I see. "

"And any girl you meet up there is either with a bloke, her parents, or a lesbian."

"Huh?"

"Yea," continued Viktor. "You know, the type who doesn't want to talk to you just because you're a single guy out trekking. The only thing they're interested in is sitting in a corner all evening writing in their diary. No interest in having a few beers and chillin' out."

I was getting slightly confused by Viktor's rationale.

"What, you mean you were trying to pick up girls trekking in the mountains?"

"No mate," grinned Viktor. "I just can't get laid anywhere!"

For the first time in weeks, I let out a laugh and a smile. So much so that I realised my mouth didn't hurt anymore. I also realised having a laugh was something I missed terribly and never knew it until just now. I reached out to shake Viktor's hand to once again thank him for bringing me something to eat. But in truth, it was to thank him for making me feel the joy of a laugh. This time, he took it and shook back.

"No worries Jonny," he grinned. "Now how about you clean up

this stinking mess and forget about all this shit and enjoy yourself a little?"

"That's not a bad idea, Viktor. Not a bad idea at all."

Once Viktor left, I opened the tub of curd he'd bought me complete with a small spoon. I stared at it and shook my head as I sniffed it. Dipping a spoon in, I tasted the slightly sour soft white thick liquid. It was yoghurt! The same stuff the old lady had been bringing me that I'd been half eating and half throwing away. The same stuff the lassie that set my stomach going was made from. Yoghurt and curd and lassi were all the same thing. I sat back before peeling a banana, slicing it up with the spoon, and then dropping the slices into the tub of curd. I had been my own worst enemy. For some reason, this didn't make me sad. It actually made me realise that I had to make a change.

CHAPTER 16

DAY ONE

Daylight was something I wasn't so accustomed to after being in a semi-conscious state in my bedroom all week. I'd also forgotten that food could actually taste good and didn't always break parts of my mouth in two. I sat eating a bacon breakfast opposite Viktor, who was quite impressed by my ability to dip bacon into fried eggs before every mouthful. My tooth felt as good as new. Though it took quite a few tender bites before I felt my shoulders relax back from the tension. The old housekeeper lady had also given my tooth a full inspection before she would allow me to leave the guesthouse.

"Chaaa," she said, holding me by the shoulders and nodding satisfactorily into my mouth.

I had no idea what she meant, but I think it was good. I pressed my two hands together and bowed a little. "Dhanyabaad."

This meant thank you in Nepali, I think. At least I heard the receptionist say it whenever someone handed over money. It seemed to work well with the old lady as she clapped in front of me before proceeding to give my head a little squeeze with her hands.

No pain, thankfully.

I also met the guesthouse owner, Ram, before I left. He was less impressed. More interested in how long I'd be staying than how my tooth was. Strange, as from my recollection, he'd been the one who made the dental appointment. Maybe he just didn't want a bad review or something.

"I gotta give them credit," quipped Viktor. "Breakfasts are good in Pokhara!"

I didn't react. Instead, I suggested we go out into Pokhara and see what the town had to offer. I mightn't like Nepal, but there was at least one old lady I did like. And she had been kinder to me than anyone else outside my family since this trip started. Even if I hadn't a clue what she was saying most of the time. Now there was Viktor.

Apparently, Viktor had only been around a couple of days since coming back from his twenty-one-day trek around the Annapurna mountains. Most of his time back in Pokhara involved eating lots of breakfast menu items and being on the lookout for girls. The latter of which he had no end of stories about. It seemed Pokhara was the place in Nepal for good looking adventure girls from Europe. It was also the place in Nepal for lots of adventure tours. Paragliding, motorbiking, river rafting, and climbing were all on offer. It wasn't a beach or an island, but it seemed an interesting way to pass the time.

Mission one for Viktor was paragliding. We went down by the shore of Lake Phewa, beside which we stayed, and watched brightly coloured paragliders float down from the high mountains that overlooked the whole of Pokhara. Each glider would swoop off the mountain in the distance. Swing over the lake before finally flying low over the lakeshore. This is when the paragliders had to make do with a landing area that was also a rice paddy and a grazing area for some meandering cattle.

"Awesome, eh?"

I looked up at an incoming paraglider. "Yea, I guess ..."

"Not chicken, are you?"

I scowled at Viktor. "No, but I do have a mouthful of stitches, you know."

"What's that got to do with paragliding?"

"Well," I started. "Incoming!"

We ducked just as a paraglider swooped in from the side and then turned sharply up towards the makeshift grass runway. It was a tandem flight where you get strapped under an experienced pilot who does all the hard work while you dangle there helplessly.

The paraglider swung low to the ground. Then lifted up again before gingerly settling down on the ground. Two figures stood while a series of belts, clasps, and shackles all fell from their torsos. There was a loud shout of joy from the passenger. A high five and all that remained was for a group of local boys to rush in and pack up the paraglider itself.

"I'm so doing that," grinned Viktor. "I wonder if there are any female instructors?"

"I'm sure there are," I replied. "Why? Fancy your chances at a romantic encounter while plunging off a mountain?"

I could actually see Viktor contemplate this a little before shaking the idea off.

"Nah, but who would you prefer to be strapped under while plunging off a mountain. Man or Woman?"

"Fair enough!" He had a point, but he also seemed to have an obsession.

Viktor seemed to be a man of his word who acted quickly. No sooner were we back on the main road than we were inside one of the many paraglider offices that dotted Lakeside. He wanted to make his first flight in the morning. I humbly offered an excuse about having a dental appointment. I wasn't sure if I was relieved or disappointed, but Viktor went on and made a booking for himself.

"One-hundred and fifty dollars?" questioned Viktor, "That's for everything?"

"Yes sir," beamed the guy behind the desk.

Viktor pulled up his shirt and proceeded to unzip his money belt. The receptionist's eyes widened as Viktor began counting out the money in crisp fifty US dollar notes. I looked down and equally felt my eyelids open wide. Viktor was flicking through a brick of US dollar notes.

"Whoa? Do you normally go around with that much on you?"

"Huh? Oh, the money," he shrugged. "No, only here."

"Isn't it a bit much to be carrying around?"

"Well, I'm not going to leave it at the guesthouse, am I? I mean, as nice as your Mama San Nepali caretaker lady is, I'm sure it wouldn't last long in my room."

I felt a little put off by that. The old lady had been nothing but nice to me. Viktor seemed to have a different take on the world. Almost an untrusting affluent take. Not a nasty one, just one that seemed like he didn't trust people very much.

"Actually, she did alright by me, Viktor," I said with conviction.

"Of course she did, mate." Viktor let loose a grin. "Only pulling your leg."

I believed him. He had just pushed the wrong button with his jibe.

We left with Viktor clutching his ticket and grinning in excitement. On our walk along Lakeside, he continued to make the odd reference in wishing for a female pilot for his flight. I was starting to figure him out. It seemed Viktor had a unique, slightly immature side. Considering we'd only known each other for a couple of days, I didn't think much of it. Then again, he only knew me as the stoned-out backpacker who burst into tears when he tried to help him out. Perhaps he was better than me regarding first impressions. He also knew more about me, after my little breakdown, than I did about him. We broke the ice over lunch.

It turns out Viktor was on the latter end of a six-month pilgrimage through India. A trip his Indian born parents had sponsored so that he could find his roots and experience what they'd gone through before moving to England. I didn't question the fact that Viktor seemed to have an unlimited supply of cash to do all this. But he didn't openly flaunt it either. Aside from the fact, it just seemed natural for him not to care about how much things cost. Yet, to his credit, he did not spend it all on fancy accommodation or high-class meals. To me, that made him an alright bloke. Although, there was still the issue of his girlfriend finding obsession. But, small steps.

The afternoon faded into an evening of Nepal Ice, a local beer, and some light bar hopping. We were searching for our 'new local'. A place we could come and sit and watch the world go by. Talk about the things we planned to do and complain about everything when things don't work out well. But best of all, a place to kick back and relax. The Busy Bee Café became that place.

Set between an indoor courtyard and an outdoor garden with a mix of low tables and high top bars, it was ideal. They served up excellent grub all day long and played something else Viktor and I had a passion for all night long. Eighties music.

"I'm thinking they only know five songs," shouted Viktor as we retreated from the local band, blasting out Bohemian Rhapsody by Queen for the third time that evening.

"Either that or they're huge Freddy Mercury fans."

The mini bar at the back of the garden where we'd sat all evening had been taken over by another group. Curiously, in Nepal, no one seemed to get completely shit-faced drunk. Or unimaginably wasted on the ample quantities of hashish that were available. Tooth repair patients aside. I put it down to the slightly expensive beer and the fact that most people were here to do some form of adventure activity. Whereas in Thailand it was cheaper to drink and easier to sit around in the sun by the sea and enjoy nearby party lifestyle activities. To corroborate this, everyone in the Busy Bee seemed to be dressed in trekking or outdoor adventure clothes. And everyone seemed to tell stories about their latest adventures. The place had a buzz about it and I was beginning to feel a little left out, not having my own trekking story.

"I think I gotta do something while I'm here." I mused openly.

"What'ya mean?" replied Viktor.

"I mean, I didn't come here to go trekking. But I kinda missed out on it too. It just seems a shame to waste any opportunities."

"World's your oyster mate. Look around. You can do just about anything you want here. Just pick something and go for it!"

"Where can we see Everest from in Pokahra?" I asked, thinking that would be a bucket list tick on many people's things to do.

"Huh?" Viktor shot me a look.

"Well, you went trekking, didn't you?"

"Yeah, mate," replied Viktor, before moving a little closer, as if he didn't want anyone to hear. "But Everest is on the other side of Nepal."

I felt stupid. I knew nothing about Nepal and had just proven it. Again, Viktor had proven himself a good chap by making sure nobody else heard my question.

"Crap," I said down cast. "Sorry, it really was a last-minute decision to come here. I didn't look much up."

"No worries," grinned Viktor. "Outside of Pokhara are the Annapurnas. Outside of Kathmandu is Everest. That's about it. There's lots more to do though if you don't want to go trekking. Look around, everyone is doing something."

I thought about that for a while. And as I did, a motorbike sped by outside. Not one of those little scooters with revved up exhausts I saw in Thailand. But a genuinely loud hardcore gas-guzzling shotgun-backfiring machine. I pointed over to the entranceway of the Busy Bee.

"That's what I'd like."

"You want to leave?"

"No, the bikes," I said, pointing at the two big bikes on display by the main door. "I've seen them around the place. Big old school bikes. I dunno. I think I've seen them rented out around some places."

"That's a Triumph," said one guy next to us at another table. "We rented a couple and drove out to some Tibetan villages."

"Awesome experience," added a girl with an Australian accent next to him.

I wondered if they'd heard my Everest remark and were feeling sorry for the new guy? But, in fairness, nobody seemed to make fun of me. They were actually offering suggestions.

Apparently, Pokhara was the place to rent old Triumph motorcycles. Or at least replicas of the famous old British bikes now made in India. Large, noisy, and very cool to ride. I was starting to like the idea.

"You can rent them?" asked one of two girls from a nearby bench like table.

"Yep," replied the first guy. "Even the ones out the front here." Then he leant in a little. "But to score a cheaper ride, just head off the main side street by the Yak Steak Café. A lot cheaper."

"Really?" chipped in Viktor. "Sounds like a bit of alright to me. What'd you think Jonny?"

I felt good about the idea. Good about doing something other than sitting around drinking and wondering what to do in a new country. A motorcycle trip in Nepal. It had a ring to it.

"Yea, I'm up for it."

"Seriously, are you guys renting some bikes?"

We both looked over at a brown-haired girl at the end of the bench as her friend turned to join us. Both had seriously tanned faces, and both were wrapped up in puffy North Face jackets. Complete with golden reflector type sunglasses placed on their heads. If you've ever seen one of those USA movies where they all go off to a winter camp skiing, then these girls would have fitted in perfectly.

With Viktor continuing to stare paralytically at the two girls. I nodded in confirmation. "Yeah, sounds like it could be a good thing."

"Cool," smiled the second girl with slightly darker hair.

Then there was that awkward silence that happens when you're all just breaking the ice and not sure if it's just a casual conversation or if there's an opening to be made. Since Viktor seemed to be lost in a world of his own, all of a sudden I took a chance.

"Wanna come?"

The two girls looked at each other. Smiled. Then, in unison confirmed and pulled their bench nearer to our table. And so we began to plan our first motorcycle trip with Amy and Beth from New Zealand. Two nursing students game on for a mini adventure. Strangely, Viktor seemed completely out of his element.

CHAPTER 17

PULLING IT TOGETHER

The dentist was impressed at how fast my tooth had recovered. I wasn't convinced, but looking at his mirror, it was hard to argue with him. As he tugged each stitch out, I felt nothing. There was no blood, pain, or other strange things falling out of my mouth. For this alone, I was happy.

"No cracking nuts with that tooth, Mr Jonny," the dentist said, waggling his head. "But after that, it's as good as new."

I rubbed my jawline and added. "No popcorn either."

"Just be avoiding the street popcorn, Mr Jonny," he confirmed, simultaneously waggling his head and finger in opposite directions. "I don't know why you tourists come all the way here and then buy cheap food from roadside vendors."

And so began a ten minute talking to about how to be a good dental tourist in Nepal from a man that obviously had little to do today. He offered me a special tooth-cleaning service, but I declined. Citing that I'd had my fill of anything tooth related for a while. But I took his card and promised that I'd give it some thought before leaving Nepal. He seemed happy with that. At least his ever waggling head did.

Leaving the surgery, I noted that this side of Pokhara seemed very different from where I stayed. I remembered little from my previous visit. Possibly due to the fact, half my jaw felt like it was falling out at the time. And that I had drunk a bottle of rum before arriving. Things were definitely different here. This side of Pokhara was more like the traffic-filled streets of Kathmandu than the tranquil lakeside area I stayed in. All along the roadsides, there were shops selling anything from boxes of used clothes to railings lined with counterfeit designer items. A pair of sequined Armani jeans spelt 'A r m a n i e' caught my attention for being particularly gaudy. Beside them was a box of slightly more tame jeans. The cost was the equivalent of about five pounds. I wasn't sure if I wanted fake jeans that were so fake the spelling was wrong on them.

Opposite all the rundown little shops along the pavement were open stalls selling even more paraphernalia. From vegetables laid out on mats to bracelets and cooking utensils. Anything and everything was for sale in a disorganised row of human enterprise. None of that stopped the locals from shopping, though. The streets were mobbed with people. They looked different to Lakeside people, too. Here women wore colourful shawls with gold or silver sequins that formed pretty patterns. I knew these were known as saris. It also seemed to me that these were more traditional garb, as mainly older ladies wore them. The younger women were more inclined to be wearing a mix of western t-shirts and fake designer anything. The men, on the other hand, were not so colourful. Older Nepali men wore grey trousers and plain shirts. Whilst the younger, cooler types wore more of the same fake designer gear.

What I noticed most were people's hair. Older ladies and men sometimes had orange streaks running through their hair. Henna dye the receptionist at my hotel told me after I asked why the old cleaner lady had orange hands. The younger girls all had long, dark, flowing hair, which was really nice. But the younger guys looked something akin to eighties movie stars with either blow-dried hair or hair with serious amounts of mousse to style it all as high as possible.

"Namaste," I jumped to the side as a man pushed a woolly hat in front of me. "Four hundred rupees!"

"No, no thank you," I replied before being pushed back towards him by a large local lady with surprising ease.

A couple of young ladies giggled at my plight through colourful scarves held up to their faces. Meanwhile, beside the hat selling man, his friend gave a big belly laugh and said something in Nepali that set all the other vendors off laughing. I tried to smile back, but it was a little difficult knowing I was at the butt of their joke. Instead, I found myself being pushed and bumped on by a huge sway of Nepali human traffic that was all elbows and shoulders.

People had no time for 'excuse me's', or 'sorry's' here. It was all bumper to bumper humanity, and no one seemed to mind. I tried the odd 'Sorry, excuse me' and 'Watch out!' but it all fell on deaf ears. It was a battle for survival just to walk along the pavements in Nepal. So I took to the road. A worse mistake.

Motorbikes whizzed by honking horns louder than most trucks. Tiny beat-up cars broke every rule in the book to avoid stopping at any junction, pedestrian crossing, or non-working traffic light. I then wondered why there were no police directing traffic under the broken lights. The large plumes of purple haze spluttering out of the mass of cars and bikes might have had something to do with it.

This was all very different to Lakeside. And I wondered why? Was lakeside just a charade put on for visiting tourists? Was this part of Pokhara, just like Kathmandu, the real Nepal?

Instead of a taxi, I walked back to Lakeside. It wasn't far and the closer I got, the fewer people seemed to be around. Maybe thirty minutes after leaving the chaos of Pokhara's 'other side' I was back listening to monk chants flowing out of little trekking shops selling colourful hand-knitted goods and counterfeit North Face gear. It was like stepping between two different worlds.

Avoiding all manner of food stalls, makeshift fruit juice vendors, and staring with rage at the little peanut and popcorn sellers along the roadside, I made my way to the Busy Bee. Viktor was due after his paragliding experience. If he'd survived. Our plan for the afternoon was to arrange our bike trip tomorrow with the New Zealand girls.

"Jonny! Over here, mate," Viktor was having a celebratory drink with some others. All looking like they'd just had a shot of adrenaline, so I presumed they were from the same paragliding trip this morning.

"So how was it?"

"Bloody outstanding!" beamed Viktor. "Flew like a bird in the clouds, Jonny. Amazing experience."

"And you landed, okay?" I asked, looking him up and down.

"Yea. I mean, it freaked me out when we flew over some old guy with a buffalo and cart. But we landed and I barely even felt it."

"Probably because you had your leg up in the air screaming like a little girl."

A round of laughter rose up after a large German-sounding guy cracked the joke and another two confirmed the girl scream. Viktor took it well, though.

"You, mate, are just jealous," he said, taking a drink. "If I recall correctly, you guys ended up in a heap on the ground. Stellar performance."

The larger of the Germans went serious for a moment before articulating his experience. "I wanted to try landing myself. The instructor didn't think I could do it, so it messed up our landing a little. I'll do it again solo next time. It will be perfect then."

"And you?" someone else asked me. "Did you try it yet?"

I shook my head, then pointed to my jaw. "No, had to have some stitches removed from my mouth this morning."

There was a rush of oh's, and ah's in amongst some squeamish looks. "Broke it when I arrived here. Good as new now though."

Then, to re-establish my credibility, I mentioned our plan to rent some motorbikes and see Nepal tomorrow. Another chorus of excitement murmured up and a few questions were asked. Not having a clue where we were going or anything, I let Viktor answer. He had a knack for making things sound better than they were. Granted, there was some exaggeration, but what the hell.

He rabbited on for a while, nearly always mentioning something about the two girls joining us.

"Speaking of Amy and Beth, have you seen them? I thought they were going to meet us here after lunch so we can go see the bikes?"

Viktor nodded nonchalantly. "Yea, they're over there I think."

Sure enough, the two girls were sitting at a table near the entranceway to the Busy Bee. I must have missed them when I came in. But it was clear as the day they'd been watching us carry on without them. I looked at Viktor and gave him a slap on the shoulder.

"What's up Vik? Didn't you say hello to them?"

"Eh, no, I only saw them come in a while ago."

"So? Did you at least wave hello?"

"I already ordered lunch over here. And ..."

"Bloody hell, mate, no wonder they look pissed off over there. Come on, let's go over."

Going into damage control, I walked straight over. They looked up at me as if I was interrupting them. "Hey, sorry, I only just arrived. Didn't see you over here."

Beth was the first to relent. "Yea, we saw you come in and over to your mate."

"Had to get my ... " I paused, then thought the better of telling them I just had stitches removed. Then again, maybe some honesty was needed. "Stitches removed."

"Stitches?"

"Yea," I said, patting my jaw. "Nasty experience with a ... stone." Okay, not one hundred percent honesty, but there was no evidence there was no stone. Besides, breaking a tooth on a corn kernel is not something one should admit openly to strangers.

" ... in a bag of popcorn," I continued. "Split my tooth pretty bad, so I got it repaired."

"Oh, you poor thing!" said Beth, turning towards me. "A stone?"

"Yea," I replied, looking concerned. "I was starving and saw this local vendor. But I guess a stone seemed to have slipped in."

I felt a small wave of guilt. But again, it could have been a stone. I nearly had myself convinced it was at this stage.

"Ouuuuch," winced Amy, brushing back her hair as I sat down opposite them.

"Yea, not a pretty experience. But you know I went to a local dentist."

"Local?" gasped Amy, taking a sip from her coke.

"Yea, it's over on the other side of Pokhara. Crazy place. Have you been?"

"There's another side?" asked Amy.

"Yea, it's like Kathmandu. Full of cars, bikes, and an army of people all selling fake Armani stuff."

"Armani?" the girls asked in unison.

"Yea, the stores over there are full of designer stuff. Gucci, Armani, Calvin Klein you name it, they've got it."

"Handbags?"

"Eh, yea I think I saw a few stores filled with bags."

"Burberry?" asked Beth, clearly getting excited over this revelation and forgetting about being miffed at me.

"Not sure," I said uncertainly. "But I'll take you there on my bike tomorrow if you want?"

"Really?" the girls smiled wildly with a strange hunger in their eyes.

"Yea, no problem. But I have to be honest with you. It's kinda rough over there. I've never seen so many people pushing and shoving. Some right dodgy people too."

The girls didn't seem worried. They were already engrossed in a side conversation about how many of what they thought would look good on somebody. Then something about someone called Tara who wouldn't be seen dead in anything by Claude.

"So like we're still on for tomorrow, yea girls?"

Amy wriggled back around to me on her seat and nodded with big blue eyes flashing a renewed interest. Of the two girls, I fully admit Amy had caught my fancy. It was also her first trip overseas, and she also struggled with Nepal at the start. But I stopped myself from thinking of anything more romantic. I just wanted to be free to enjoy myself on a good road trip. And it was good to meet new people who wanted to do the same.

Both of them seemed genuinely nice. Not too wild for two nurses taking a time out to go trekking. They both sported dark hair and an equal fashion sense for the Alpine look. The biggest difference between them is that Amy had wild blue eyes while Beth had dark brown eyes. Both girls still seemed to be up for a motorbike tour of Pokhara and were genuinely interested in what type of bikes we'd be getting. That, in my book, made them adventurous and just the sort of people I needed to make Nepal worth the visit.

"Is your mate still coming, though?"

Beth looked over at Viktor across the Busy Bee. He was still talking it up with his group of paragliding buddies. For all his talk of girls, he was really letting the side down over here.

"Yea, no probs," I said, trying to make excuses for him. "He just went paragliding today and is on a serious adrenaline rush if you know what I mean."

"Wow, really?"

"Yea," I said, knowing my excuse might just work. It was time to get Viktor to come over. "Hey, Viktor! Stop yakking about your perfect landing and come over here. We've got some bikes to rent."

Viktor looked over and smiled in a sort of cocky I'm a movie star way. Only the smile didn't go away. He just stood there beaming over at us as if frozen in time.

"Hello?" I waved.

He snapped out of his trance. Picked up his glass of beer, nodded at the others and gave them a big thumbs up. Once over by us, he sat down and just smiled.

An awkward silence followed.

"So Viktor, I was just telling Amy and Beth about your awesome paraglide today."

Viktor looked up at the two girls with a grin. Then mumbled something inaudible.

"Sorry?" said Beth, moving closer.

Viktor mumbled again. This time something like, "Amazing experience," came out of his mouth.

"Cool, did you go solo or tandem?" asked Amy.

"Tandem."

"Really, first time?"

Viktor's forehead was starting to produce a thin line of perspiration as he nodded another confirmation. I suddenly got the impression, despite his talk, Viktor was not so good around the opposite sex.

"He's still recovering," I said, going into damage control again. "It was a big thing for him. Having acrophobia and all. Today he just beat his fear of heights!"

"Wow, that's so awesome, mate," cooed Beth, slapping the table. "You totally rock for doing that."

The girls smiled in wait for a response while Viktor looked over at me blankly and then back at Beth with a grin similar to a little shy schoolboy.

Bloody heck, there was no doubt about it. Viktor was clearly terrified.

None of this newfound discovery about Viktor was evident when we went to the motorbike shop to enquire about renting a couple of Triumphs for the day. It was cheap. Well compared to the UK. About fifty pounds, not including petrol. This is when yet another side of Viktor stepped up with some impressive bartering.

"I want to see receipts," he said to the big-bellied Nepali man we were renting the bikes from. "And I want your phone number in case we get punctures. And, I just want to be sure, you will come out and fetch us if one of the bikes breaks down without charge?"

"Yes, sir. No problem sir." said the big-bellied man with a waggle of his shaven head.

"Yea mate, but I want it in writing alright?" continued Viktor, looking for something more conclusive.

It all took an extra thirty minutes, but Viktor did just that. He had just ensured that our day would go smoothly, no matter what. And he got it all in writing. Even if he did have to write it all out on the back of the receipt. It became clear Viktor knew a thing or two about business, contracts, and possibly renting bikes. The two girls wanted to hire their own bike and share it between them to save some money. My laddish image of us both riding with a girl behind us along mountain roads quickly vanished. That was a fantasy, this was reality.

Viktor again came up trumps as the girls tried taking turns getting on a red sports bike with some difficulty. It was too tall for them.

"Better off on one of these," he said, pulling over a souped-up looking silver scooter.

"A moped!" frowned Amy.

"Yea, it's really a lot safer if there are two of you on one of these. I mean, if you want to go solo, then by all means take one of the sports bikes or even a Triumph like us. But these mopeds they use here are a lot safer on these roads, if you know what I mean?"

The two girls looked at each other and then talked about the cost. The moped was cheaper. By far. Done deal.

I saw my chance to offer a compromise. "But if you guys want to try out our bikes when we're out tomorrow, then I've no problem swapping."

Amy looked over and saw me patting my cream and navy Triumph Classic. "Really?"

"Sure, no problem," I smiled.

"Cool!"

Mission accomplished. All that remained was to get Viktor pried away from adjusting something on one bike. And then get him to talk about something else other than kickstands and rev counters. I suggested we ask the girls out to one of the steak houses around lakeside later.

I waited for Viktor to offer the suggestion. I waited a bit longer. And waited some more. Finally, the girls gave up standing around and said they'd see us in the morning before walking away arm in arm.

"What's up, man?" I said, throwing my arms out to the side.

"What?"

"Why didn't you ask em' out for dinner later?"

Silence.

"Just biding my time," he said, patting his bike. "They are into me. I just gotta show them I'm cool with it."

"Eh?" I gasped. What planet was Viktor from? I didn't get it.

Maybe Viktor was just having a laugh with me. But after his sit down session of silence earlier, I had a suspicion; it was the complete opposite of what he said. As we strolled along lakeside looking for a place for dinner, sans Amy and Beth, I wondered if he would choke again tomorrow? Or would he shine through on the bikes as we take to the mountain roads of Nepal?

CHAPTER 18

ROADTRIP

We stocked up on pizza slices, sausage rolls, banana cake, chocolate rolls, and chocolate chip cookies from the Swiss bakery. This was another big plus for Nepal. They had excellent bakeries. All of these were packed into the ample storage compartment of Amy and Beth's scooter. Viktor had a day pack filled with coke, water, and a packet of ... condoms. He insisted that he should buy condoms last night. I tried to explain to him we would be on motorbikes all day. But he came back with a big grin about how romance would fill the day instead. Of course, when the girls showed up, he shied away into silence again. We jumped on the bikes and after a few false starts and the odd wobble; we were off. All of a sudden, life was starting to feel good again.

The two Triumph motorcycles made a noise similar to mini shotgun blasts as we revved them up high. Motorcycles like this would have been banned in the UK due to everything from emissions to noise to the fact they were probably breaking every safety rule in modern-day mechanics. There was something mildly rebellious about it all. A smile drew across my face as I reached into my chest pocket, pulled out one of my pre-made joints from the time with my tooth. Then, felt half of it disintegrate against the wind as

I held it up to my mouth. How did this work so well in the movies? But even with that notion, I felt stupid. I remembered Thailand. I remembered the bad trip. Then, with some strange satisfaction, I loosened my lips and let the rest of it blow away into the wind.

I didn't need it. The sky above was blue. To our right were snow-capped mountains and to our left a beautiful still water lake. There was no traffic on the road apart from the odd local bike and some occasional farmers walking.

Now and then, there was a little honk of a horn as Amy and Beth's moped revved up beside us. Beth was driving with huge fifties-style goggles and looked to have a permanent smile etched across her petite face. Amy behind her was riding pillion and had her hands outstretched. I raised my fist up into the air and hollered.

Amy let out a huge "Whooooooooo!"

We followed the road around Lake Phewa, slowing down only if we saw a gap in the mountains that offered us views of the Annapurna range. Locals waved hellos at us and we waved back or honked our outrageously loud horns back at them. Finally, after a couple of hours, Viktor pulled over by a lush green rice paddy.

"Bloody heck, I'm starving. Think we can stop for a bite?" he asked.

Unloading everything from the girl's scooter, we set up a mini picnic area using two shawls the girls had packed away. I made some mild adjustments to the paper plates and tissue wrapped pizzas so I could get a good view of the mountains. Meanwhile, Viktor sat with his back to Beth and just stared out at the rice paddy with a huge snowcapped mountain behind it.

For the first time, Amy nudged her elbow against mine. She nodded towards Viktor and then looked quizzical. I didn't know how to react. If Viktor didn't get his act together, it was going to sour our day. I did the only thing a self-respecting friend would do.

"Hey Viktor, tell us about your trip to India?"

"Sure."

Viktor broke out into a huge smile and leaned back on the sari beside Beth. "You know," he began. "I don't like to brag, but it was easy to travel there for me."

Well, it was a start. Our time passed munching on tasty bakery goodies and questioning Viktors' adventures in India. Particularly whenever he mentioned meeting a beautiful girl. This seemed to happen a lot whenever he was on a train for some reason. Each time he'd enter a compartment, there would be this beautiful girl. Nothing ever happened, but it made us laugh all the same whenever he mentioned a train to some place great.

"Nothing," remarked Viktor. "Compares to getting on a train to Varanasi from Delhi. I got upgraded to first class, you know? This happens in India a lot if there are spaces. They fill up first class randomly so more people will buy second-class tickets."

"Anyway," he continued. "I went into my two person cabin, and there sitting on the lower bunk was the most beautiful ."

"Girl!" joked Amy and Beth in unison.

"Absolutely," beamed Viktor. "I mean, of all the trains and carriages and cabins, I'd be sharing with someone so radiant all night long."

"Okay," I chipped in, "and the rest is x-rated, I guess?"

Everyone laughed. Though, Viktor seemed to mull the thought over a little too much. Thankfully, the conversation moved on.

"So where should we head after this?" Beth asked.

I was about to suggest we try visiting a small village, but Viktor got there first. "I hear there's a Tibetan refugee camp somewhere around here."

"Cool." Beth was interested.

Good. We had a plan.

"We could visit that and see what it's like to get kicked out of your own country." Viktor continued.

"Yea, it's a horrible situation," said Beth.

"And the world doesn't give a crap!"

"I'm totally with you, man," agreed Beth, taking a sip from Viktor's coke.

"About time," I whispered to Amy.

"Takes a while for your buddy to warm up, I think?"

"Something like that I guess." I replied. At least Viktor was a little more into the conversation today.

"We know what to do in the future, eh?" she said in a low whisper. "Ask him to talk about himself."

I blurted out a chuckle and looked out at the lake on the opposite side of the road.

"Well, maybe we'll all have a new story after today."

Beth nodded as she also looked at the lake that now reflected the snow-capped mountains. "You know," she said, "that's a good point. I guess we all do the same thing in our own way."

We must have sat there for an hour chilling out. Eating cold pizza, drinking coke, and talking about where we were all going next. For once, I didn't like the idea of planning. I just wanted to live in the moment. When Amy mentioned she was thinking of going white water rafting all the way back to Kathmandu, I thought it was a great idea. Better yet, was Beth's plan after that to go on a wildlife safari in Chitwan National park. There suddenly seemed so much more to Nepal than I'd originally thought.

We stayed much longer due to Viktor suddenly opening up and talking about how he had two bikes in London and how he actually hated India so much. Apparently, Viktor had no intention of getting in touch with his roots like his parents had wanted. He'd spent two of his four months in India chilling out in Goa. Two more months staying with relatives in a rather upmarket apartment in New Delhi. He'd then hopped on a train. Spent a night in Varanasi before hiring a jeep to escape up to Nepal. Once again, he wasn't so happy here as it had a similar vibe, but at least he wasn't constantly asked for money by relatives or complete strangers. It seemed to be an Indian from England, and returning to India was not such an easy thing to do.

"The heat, the flies, and the beggars," he contemplated. "I really don't know how anyone could stick it there for long.

"I mean, don't get me wrong. I know people have a shit life there. But why do I have to go back there? I'm not from there. I'm from Putney."

Beth offered an answer. "Maybe your parents just wanted you to see what life could have been like?"

"But it's not. Know what I mean?" he rebuked. "I know what shit is like. I see it in London too. Homeless people. Drunks. Addicts. The lot. They're there too. I don't need to go to India to see all that. If it were me, I'd prefer to help people back home. Just because they were born there doesn't mean I have to pretend I was too. I'm English, not Indian."

"Fair enough," said Beth, who seemed to be genuinely agreeing with him. "No one should force you to be something you're not."

"Dead right," Viktor replied. "That's why I came to Nepal. I didn't know anything about the place until I bought a guidebook and researched about it. I then went trekking by myself. I can handle hardship. I just want to do things my own way."

"I thought you hired a guide?" I butted in.

Viktor raised his eyes to heaven. "Yea mate, no worries. The guide came with me 'cause I wanted to chill out and enjoy the scenery an' all."

"Cool," nodded Beth, who began packing things up.

It was time to move on. But the stop had been worth it. Viktor had opened up and was actually, at long last, conversing with the opposite sex. Meanwhile, I'd got to know everyone a little better. For the first time since my first year in university, I was completely happy going slow. I was making new friends and getting to know something more about a new old friend, too. We also seemed to have new travel ideas forming together, which sounded excellent.

Our Tibetan village visit was filled with old ladies weaving blankets and sewing blankets. The girls took photos and the old ladies were quick to hold out their hands, looking for money. I was of two minds if giving money to them helped or whether it only encouraged begging. In the end, Beth gave them a few small notes. It was enough to stop them from asking, but not enough to make us stop feeling guilty for taking photos. Except that is for Viktor, who sided heavily on the don't give them anything rational. Thinking all this could quickly turn into a hasty debate, I suggested riding until the end of the road around the far side of the lake before going into the built-up side of Pokhara for some counterfeit designer-ware shopping. The deal was made, and we headed off from our brief encounter with Tibetan culture.

The surrounding mountains were now mixed with lush green landscapes and fleeting views of the lake. All evidence of a country that had a natural harmony. The end of the road was the start of a local trek known as Panchase Peak. We stopped by a local store for some lemon sodas and mused over the idea of going on a trek together. There wasn't time today. But the idea seemed more appealing now than before. It was only a two-day trek, but at least I could say that I'd been trekking. The others agreed. I suddenly began looking forward to things again. We took off back down the road on our bikes to explore the other side of Pokhara.

As we got closer to the city, the road became a mixture of concrete and tarmacadam. Strangely, it also became dustier and harsher compared to the country roads. It all resembled a sort of no-man's-land before the heavy traffic, local stores, and mass of humanity appeared.

"Bloody hell," yelled Beth. "What's with all the traffic?"

"Welcome to the other side of Pokhara," I shouted back. "Keep your cool and stay close."

Of course, this was all talk. I was more nervous than ever on a motorbike in amongst all the local bikes, bicycles, rickshaws, and little beaten up cars. I followed Viktor, who was far more confident, as we kept as close to the side of the road as possible. It meant we avoided all the interweaving traffic and crazy three cars to one lane style of driving. But it also meant we had to cope with the odd person wandering out from an overflowing footpath of makeshift stalls.

Viktor suddenly lurched to the side and let out a blast of his horn as a small boy ran out in front of him. Then he braked hard as a skinny goat ran after the boy. Each one dodged the oncoming stream of traffic like it was a natural reflex action.

I caught a glimpse of some stores selling clothes and signalled to the others. They weren't the same stalls as yesterday. It wasn't even the same road. Truth be told, I had no clue where we were as there wasn't a signpost in sight. How anyone knows where anything is seems a like mystery in Nepal.

Viktor pulled over beside a man selling grapes from a glass trolley like contraption. A series of motorbikes honked past us. Each one not even looking at us. Just blasting their horns for the hell of it.

"Is this it then?" shouted Amy over the din.

I looked over at a row of clothes shops and spotted some denim jeans that looked like designer garb. Viktor offered to mind the bikes as we took on the assault course of trying to get from the side of the road to the stores themselves over a pavement filled with a sea of bustling humanity.

"Don't' be worried about pushing past," I called out after getting what felt like a sharp elbow in the back from someone. "They all do it."

The girls didn't seem to notice. They were already in the second store by the time I'd made it across. More Armani clothes than you could possibly ever expect to see swallowed them up inside the shop. I couldn't figure out why all the clothes shops all sold the same brands and styles. I'm guessing at the same prices too. Why didn't someone offer up something a little different from the store next door? And why did all the women insist on looking inside both stores selling the same items?

Unfortunately, Amy and Beth were none too impressed with what I thought was designer gear. Something to do with looking too fake. There was a brief moment of excitement at the sight of a Burberry handbag. But once they'd got through pulling and tugging at it, disappointment followed.

"It's really rough, Johnny," Amy said, holding up a pair of 'Calvin Klein' jeans. One leg looking a little longer than the other.

"I never really gave them that much of a look," I said, trying to distance myself from the gear. "Not really much of a shopper you know."

The girls looked at each other and nodded in agreement.

"Early drinks at the Bee then?" Beth offered.

Amy tossed the jeans back. "First round is on you Jonny?"

"No worries if the second is on you?" I replied.

Damage control wasn't needed. The girls had enjoyed our day out as much as I did. The smile on Viktor's face indicated it was a good day all around. We followed the girls back to the bike shop, then walked them to their guesthouse for a quick shower before agreeing to meet up again at the Busy Bee for dinner.

"You think Beth wants to shag me tonight, then?"

"You what mate?" I said in shock at Viktors' question, nearly spilling my beer in the process. "You barely said a word to her all day until you started up about India. What makes you think she wants to sleep with you?"

"She's into me," replied Viktor, as if it was obvious. "Can't you tell?"

"That's why you stink of cologne, then?"

Viktor sat up and sniffed at his freshly pressed red pinstriped shirt. "Not too much, is it?"

"Do you really get the cleaning lady to iron all your shirts?" I asked in jest. Viktor took it seriously.

"What? No. I have them sent out."

"Really?"

"Yea, of course. It's my style man."

"What is?"

"Looking fresh. I mean, look around. All these backpackers, hikers, and what have you. They all look a bit rough, you know what I mean?"

"No," I said, looking down at my own slightly wrinkled t-shirt.

"Naw, mate. Not you. I mean yeah, you're a bit rough and all."

"What?"

"No, what I mean is, everyone here looks like a traveller. Because that's what they're doing. Me, I'm travelling too. But my 'thing' is I also look pretty mean and stylish. I look like I do back home. I figure that's what the girls like. A bit of clean refinement an' all."

"Interesting theory."

"Well, he does look very clean and proper."

Viktor let loose a bashful pearly white smile at Beth. The two girls had arrived and were dressed up like they were out on the town in London. Amy wearing a little black dress with a black denim jacket. Beth in red jeans and a green low cut top that had Viktor transfixed.

"Nice one girls, sit down." I laughed. "First rounds on me if I remember."

We laughed, drank, ate a delicious pizza, and moved over to the band area as the nightly eighties cover versions had started up. When it all became a bit much and Viktor began threatening to start dancing, we moved to the back of the bar to some of the lounge chairs. Amy was by now permanently by my side and enjoying my stupid jokes about eighties rock bands and the need for better dentists in Nepal. We also began planning for this epic rafting trip back to Kathmandu after a short trek to Panchase Peak. Meanwhile, Beth and Viktor seemed to hit it off, too. Mainly over conversations about Tibet and human rights issues. Not my thing, but it seemed to work for them. Amy moved in closer as the night air began getting cooler. I just sat back and relaxed. I wasn't pushed for anything. I was just enjoying my newfound lease on travel and new friends.

"Jonny! Is that you?"

My mouth dropped.

"Anne?"

"Jonny?"

Fuck.

CHAPTER 19

CRASHING BACK TO THE OLD WORLD

"What's up then?"

I looked up and barely recognised Anne. Her face was bright red and her hair was wildly frizzy, as if she'd just jumped out of a plane. Behind her Benji, the monk appeared. He only smiled when Anne turned around to him.

"Just chillin' back, Anne," I replied, still in a little shock. "Erm, when did you get back?"

"Today," she said, plonking her handbag down on the table. Her once prized and pristine handbag now had a series of stains, roughed up edges and a line of black grime along the bottom edge. "What's all this then? New friends?"

"Erm, yea. This is …"

"Lovely. Benji's introduced me to some great people at an orphanage nearby too."

"Really?"

"Yea, it's been an amazing experience with Benji."

"Where's Stuart then?"

"Stuart? He's somewhere up near Manang, I think?"

"Didn't it work out then or something?"

"What?"

I could see I'd already offended her. I genuinely wondered why they didn't come back together. All the same, I found it rude she interrupted me when I was introducing everybody. But I held back and continued in curiosity.

"I mean, I thought you guys were trekking together?"

"Well," Anne snipped back. "Stuart is going to a lost kingdom. I just went to Poon Hill and came back with Benji. That was the plan, if you remember?"

Whether it was the alcohol kicking in, the annoyance, or the fact that it was a blatant lie, I couldn't let the last bit slip by unnoticed.

"No. I never heard the plan. If you remember I broke my tooth, and then you left. And by the way, my tooth is doing fine. Thank you for asking."

"Yea the popcorn, I remember."

"I thought you chipped it on a stone?" quipped Beth.

"I did," I replied, remembering my previous omission. "A stone in a bag of popcorn."

"Burnt popcorn kernels can be like stones." confided Amy.

"Yea, they can be," I said, slightly taken aback by Amy's defence of me.

"Right," concluded Anne. She let loose a bitter, tight-lipped smile at me before she panned around at the others.

"Poon Hill must have been nice?" offered Amy.

"Yea, lovely," replied Anne as Benji the monk offered her up a chair.

I sat up and sacrificed some introductions again. The worst mistake of the night. It only brought up too many questions with Anne back and it wasn't long before the worst of the worst conversation came about.

"So how do you two know each other?" said Amy, looking a little confused.

"We went to Uni together," I replied, thinking up of something to change the conversation. "Anyone want another drink?"

"And you came here together?" asked Beth.

This was getting bad. I glared at Viktor for some support. Distracting Beth from interrogatory questions would have been nice.

"Yea," nodded Anne, "Just the two of us. But you know, we all make mistakes, don't we?"

Fuck. What was she saying? Anne was on the verge of hitting the self-destruct button. There was an awkward silence as people began to digest what she meant.

"You mean you two are a couple?" Amy finally asked, looking like a scolded solicitor.

"No never," denied Anne. "Forget it. I have. It's all in the past, eh Jonny?"

I sat back and realised that Anne had set about stirring up as much shit in my direction as she could. She still wanted blood for my mistake in Thailand. This was yet another way to make me suffer, it seemed. But enough was enough. Anne seemed mightily happy in Nepal and didn't think twice about dumping me here when I really needed someone. No more.

"Yea Anne, it's in the past. So why don't we just drop it, eh?"

"Drop what?"

"Give it a rest."

"You're the one who got caught for possession in Thailand."

"What? I never?"

"Did you get arrested or not?"

"No," I said, pushing my beer back in anger. "A fucking Thai cop saw me smoking weed and tried to bust me. We bribed him and ended up here because our visas ran out. And because Stuart was coming here."

"Leave Stuart out of it?"

"Why? Because he dumped you after your trek?"

"What?! Screw you, Jonny! Nothing ever happened with Stuart."

"Yeah right, you had the fucking hots for him since you met him in Bangkok."

"You're sick."

"I'm sick? You're the one who dumped me to come all the way over here to meet him again."

"Okaaaay!" said Amy, moving to one side. "Look, sorry guys, but this is all a bit much for me."

"What? Wait," I pleaded, looking over at Amy as she stood up and walked over to Beth.

"Yea, it was nice guys," grimaced Beth, "but we really don't think this has anything to do with us. And, we are not into the drug scene when travelling."

"Yea, sorry Jonny," smiled Amy with an upturned lip. "But this is a bit much. We'll see you guys around, okay."

My shoulders slumped, and I slouched into the chair. I watched as the two girls grabbed their coats and walked slowly out of the Busy Bee. Everything had just collapsed in the space of five minutes.

"Bit touchy aren't they?" Anne said, shrugging.

"Oh, fuck off Anne."

"Fuck you, Jonny." Anne clenched her jaw. "I only told the truth."

I sat up and glared at her. Then noticed Benji the Monk moving closer as if he had suddenly become a bodyguard. Viktor, for the first time in all this, also sat up to counter Benji moving in.

Anne let loose a laugh. "What, you need your mate here to back you up, do you?"

"Huh," I replied, a bit unsure about what was happening. "He's watching the monk."

"What? You think Benji is going to suddenly launch himself across the table and head butt you or something?"

She looked back at Benji. He smiled. Then when she turned back to me, his smile dropped, and he glared at us. Something was way off with this monk. He gave me the creeps.

"Just give it a rest, Anne," I said, taking a drink. "The damage is done tonight. You've had your revenge. Now just drop it, please."

Anne threw up her hands, stood up, and turned to walk away. Benji the monk following closely on her heels. I knew she could be spiteful. I knew that from growing up and visiting Charles. She'd always thrown out sarcastic quips at me and anyone else that dared to talk against her views. I should have known if it became personal, things would be worse. Which they had. Now it was all boiling over.

"So that's your ex, eh?" quipped Viktor as we watched Anne and Benji leave the Busy Bee.

"Yea that's Anne. Piece of fucking work, eh?"

"Never saw anything like it, mate."

"Tell me about it."

"Massive tits though."

"What? Jeez, Viktor get a life!"

We bought a bottle of Jack Daniels and a bucket of ice. Despite all this. Viktor was still here. He could have gone with the girls. It was my fault the night was ruined. Our new friends were gone, but here we remained. Pouring a glass each of whiskey we agreed to wash away every trace of the past five minutes by any means necessary. If only the same could be said for Anne.

***

The sound of guttural hacking of phlegm woke me up. I was lying near face down on my pillow. I'd been drooling in my sleep, but my mouth was as dry as sandpaper. Something didn't quite feel right. The world was slightly distant. I tried to swallow and my tongue scrapped along the back of my mouth like a dry weight. I gagged a little and sat up. Big mistake. My heart began to beat a little faster as my stomach felt like it just hit the floor. Then my eyes began thumping to the beat of my heart, soon followed by a visceral pain shooting through my temples. It all came back in one swoop. The taste of Jack Daniels rose up from my stomach. My nose was clogged with bar smoke and my clothes felt dank.

I reached for my backpack and pulled out my first aid kit. The only thing I'd ever used from it was paracetamol. I took two and stood up to wash my face. There's always a few tender moments when you wonder how bad the hangover is going to be. Will it be a thumping headache for the day? Or a morning of throwing up? Or the weird third option of still being slightly drunk and feeling just fine. I had the former. A pounding headache.

The best cure for this type of headache was a full-on breakfast. I looked at my watch. 11.30am. Okay, it's Nepal, all-day breakfasts are normal. Bacon, eggs, coffee, and I'd be fine. I tried a hot shower first to try and wake up a little better. That's when flashbacks from the night before started.

The New Zealand girls, the bikes, the dinner. Anne … The conversation was muggy but not so bad to not remember it all. What a spiteful person she was last night. Spiteful and vengeful. The worse thing was that it already hurt when she just up and left after I broke my tooth. No concern at all. So what if we weren't in a relationship anymore? What friend would just dump another in a strange country only they wanted to see and then go off trekking with another guy?

She deliberately came over last night and set about dismantling my credibility in front of Viktor and, more specifically, the two girls. Why? What type of person would do that? I wondered what would happen next? She mentioned something last night about doing something with Benji the monk, but I couldn't recall it over my headache.

I came out of the bathroom feeling a lot better. My room looked worse off than me, judging by the heaps of clothes strewn around the place. The idea of doing a clothes wash fleeted across my mind. Then I remembered I'd only just done one a few days ago. My eyes darted over to the small table in the corner of the room. There were some books over there, and my phone, but no laptop!

A mild sense of panic filled me as I dived under the desk in search of its case. I always left it on top of the table. Did I use it last night? I threw back the bedsheets, looking for any trace of it. But only found my day pack, lying there opened. I looked inside. No laptop, but my passport was there. My phone charger was there, along with a bundle of cash and a backup phone. But no laptop.

I must have lifted up all the clothes that were strewn around the room in search of it. All the time questioning myself if I'd used it last night or not. Had I given it to Viktor last night? Maybe that was it? Yes, that must have been it. He'd been asking to borrow it to watch some movie. Maybe in my drunken stupor last night I'd just reached in and given it to him before passing out? He was probably hungover and sitting downstairs eating a cure too.

Finding my keys still in my pocket, I hurriedly got dressed. Pushing aside some clothes on the floor by the door, I reached over to the handle nearly stepping on a small piece of paper lying on the ground. My name was written across the fold. I recognised the handwriting and opened it up.

> *Jonny,*
> *Gone to KTM to volunteer with Benji at a monastery*
> *for orphans.*
> *Peace,*
> *Anne.*

Peace?! What the hell? She'd up and left again! This time to some unknown orphanage in Kathmandu. What was she thinking? Where was she? Where was the orphanage? Did her brother, Charles, know?

I scrunched up the paper note and made my way downstairs. My hangover was slipping away and was being replaced by anger, betrayal, and utter confusion. Viktor was slouching by a table near the window of the guesthouse cafe, looking quite pale.

"She's buggered off to Kathmandu!"

"Aww, jeez, mate," groaned Viktor, rubbing his face. "I was nearly nodding off there. Some night last night, eh?"

"Didn't you hear me?"

"Wha …"

"Anne, she's buggered off to Kathmandu with the monk."

"Really?"

"Yea, left me this note under the door."

Viktor unfolded the crumpled up piece of paper, read it and shrugged. "Okay then. She's gone." He then looked at me like a true mate would when you know they are trying to be honest with you about something you don't like. "Look mate, it's probably for the best you know. I mean, after what she pulled last night."

I sat down and ordered breakfast. "It's not as simple as that, Vik. Even if she and I aren't together. She's still one of my mate's sisters. And I'm kinda meant to be looking after her, you know?"

"Yea, but like she's pissed off on you, man. Like, twice now."

"Three times if you include Bangkok at the start."

"See what I mean?"

"Yea, but this is … This is different. I mean, I don't even know what bloody monastery she's gone to? What if her brother Charles asks where she is? What am I meant to say?

"Yea, Charles, mate, she's in some monastery in that shit hole I wrote to you about last time called Kathmandu. What's that? No mate, no idea which one it is."

"So you're just worried her brother is going to deck you for losing his sister."

"No."

"Yea, you are."

"No! It's just not right. That's all. She buggers off like this and doesn't even tell me where exactly she is. Typical fucking Anne.

Same shit as last night. She's doing all this on purpose."

Breakfast arrived, and I was no better. The more I thought about Anne getting up and leaving for Kathmandu with no address to find her, the angrier I got. Add last night's performance on top of that and I'd really had enough.

"Message her brother and tell him what she's done," offered Viktor.

I thought about it and shook my head. Without knowing exactly where she was, it was like admitting I'd not looked after her properly. Then, as the hangover effects washed away with the help of breakfast and some strong Nepali coffee, another idea popped into my head. "Maybe she sent me a message with the address of the Monastery?"

"Long shot, but yea, maybe."

It wasn't beyond the realms of possibilities. Maybe she'd written a long email with all the details and addresses of where she'd be because she thought I'd lose it on a handwritten piece of paper. It started to make sense.

"Okay, yea. I better check." I said, trying to convince myself of a slim chance and remembering I'd left my phone upstairs. "Do you have my laptop somewhere down here, Viktor? I need to check my mail."

"Laptop?"

"Yea mate, didn't I give it to you last night?"

"No?"

"No?!"

"When could you have? I went straight to bed after we got back last night."

My head pounded even harder. We both went up to my room and searched in vain.

"It's gone. My laptop's gone."

"Shit mate," replied Viktor. "I told you not to leave your shit around like this."

Viktor was right. Someone had stolen my laptop.

CHAPTER 20

REALISATIONS AND CHANGES

Things move slowly in Nepal. Very slowly. There's even a Nepali song called "slowly, slowly". There's also an efficiency issue. Efficiency simply doesn't exist in Nepal. Exaggerating much? Not in the least. Here's an example. Once both Viktor and I searched my room together for the missing laptop, there was no doubt it was gone. Between us, we could also just about recall everything the night before. We'd arrived back at roughly one in the morning and gone straight to bed. It was that simple. Between leaving on our motorbike ride and coming back, someone had come in and taken the laptop. There was simply no other alternative. But, try telling that to a Nepali receptionist who really didn't seem to care about his job.

"No sir, maybe you take it with you on the motorcycle." said the receptionist matter-of-factly while he stared at me with not a care in the world.

"No, I left it on my desk," I replied, getting annoyed at the slightly insulting excuse the receptionist had offered.

The receptionist had never been that bright. A guy in his twenties called Tenga, who spent most of his day watching YouTube on a cracked mobile screen. The remaining part of the day, he had

165

an earpiece stuck in one ear and at the other end constantly flicked through his phone, smiling and laughing. In between all this 'work' he also takes orders from the guesthouse restaurant and checks a few people in when he can look up from his phone. Now he just seemed in denial that two guests confirmed a laptop theft.

"No sir, then maybe it is in your room."

"We both searched the room. Twice," I snarled, getting increasingly annoyed. "I left it on my desk in the morning, and now it's gone."

"And what about last night when you came back? Was it there?"

"I don't know, I didn't look."

"Maybe you took it out?"

"What?! That makes no sense?"

"What doesn't sir?"

"I didn't leave my room after I came back!"

"So you didn't check to see if the laptop was there, sir?"

"No! Why should I? I didn't check to see if my backpack was there either."

"So, the backpack is missing too?"

I backed off in frustration. Getting more convinced no one could be this dense and that it might well be a ruse if a member of staff had stolen my laptop when we'd been out. Viktor seemed a lot more level-headed.

"Mr Tenga," he said, tapping the reception desk. "Let's be quite certain about all this. Jonny left here yesterday morning, and the laptop was on the desk. He got back late last night and went to sleep. I saw him enter the room and lock it myself. Then this morning he discovered the laptop was missing. Are we clear?"

"Yes sir, the laptop is missing."

"Eureka!" I threw my hands up. "So what are you going to do about it?"

"Well sir, I will have to call the guesthouse owner and report it to him, sir."

"Okay, that's Ram, and the police?"

"No sir, Mr Ram is not with the police."

"Yes, I know!" I bit my lip. "I mean, shall we call the police!"

The receptionist's face dropped a little. "No sir, let me tell the owner first. We can take this very unfortunate incident from there."

"Fine."

I turned to Viktor and shook my head. "This really sucks. Between this and Anne last night I really want to get the hell out of here."

"Oh, sir," interrupted the receptionist. "About your friend Ms Anne."

"What about her?"

"She never took the receipt for her payment last night."

"What payment?"

"Her room sir. She paid and left but didn't take the receipt".

"So? Nothing to do with me, mate."

"Really? I don't know, sir. I thought you were together?"

"No, we're not!"

"Oh, I see sir." There was a moment of silence before the morning's antics jumped up a level. "But I believe you arrived together, yes?"

"Yea, we were travelling together. But not anymore."

"Ah, yes, sir. Okay, sir." replied Tenga before the penny drop statement. "That is why she picked up her things from your room yesterday then."

"What?!" My face scrunched up in mental agony. "She was in my room?"

Still clueless, the receptionist waggled his head. "Why yes, of course? She said her bags were in there."

A faint memory lit up in my head about being stuck on the toilet after the dentist when Anne came in to leave her bags.

"And you let her in?"

"Yes sir, of course. She said you were minding her bags when she went trekking."

"Bloody hell mate," winced Viktor. "You don't think … ?"

My heart sank even lower.

"Did anyone go with her into the room?" asked Viktor.

"Of course sir, she went with the housekeeper and her friend."

"What friend?"

"A monk I believe, sir?"

I tried putting logic to all this. Why would Anne have taken my laptop? Maybe she thought it was compensation for the Thailand incident? The way she carried on last night, anything was possible in her mind's eye, it seemed.

Viktor again tried to make sense of this. "Is the housekeeper around? We can ask her if she saw the laptop in the room."

Things went from sensible to illogical again. The old housekeeper lady arrived later on with the guesthouse owner, Ram. They confirmed that the housekeeper had gone with Anne and Benji the Monk to my room and let them in, as was the security policy of the guesthouse. But the greatest non-sensible thing of all was that she never went inside my room. The dear old lady said she didn't want to intrude on my privacy and mentioned multiple times that the tall lady was with a monk. A holy man that she wouldn't dare offend by following him into a room.

Ram then asked the obvious question. Had we asked Anne if she'd borrowed my laptop? We shook our heads and were politely told that maybe we should do that first before accusing anyone else.

He was right, of course. The only problem was that we had no idea where Anne was other than she was in a monastery slash orphanage in Kathmandu. I could send her a message on my phone. But even wording the question seemed like evoking trouble.

We sat in the Busy Bee over a cold beer for the rest of the day. Viktor was hoping the two New Zealand girls would make an appearance. Meanwhile, I was lost in a world of utter plight. How had things come to this? And what the hell was I to do?

"She's gone too far with this shit, Viktor," I said, shaking my head for the umpteenth time. "I mean, what the hell. First the entire relationship farce.

"Then the let's go to Chiang Mai in Thailand while not taking joint responsibility in our visas expiring. And let's not thank Jonny for giving up on South East Asia because I buggered off to Nepal.

"And let's not help a mate out when he's in the middle of fucking nowhere with a broken tooth. So let's piss off bloody trekking with some knob head and a monk.

"Only to come back. Be a spiteful bitch and fucking steal my bloody fucking laptop!!"

Viktor looked around the Busy Bee to see if others were looking at my outburst. They were. I was loud. And pissed off.

"It's a dirty deal, Jonny," Viktor said, trying to calm me down. "You've had a bad couple of weeks."

"Months! A bad couple of months," I repeated before taking a mouthful of beer and swallowing it with authority. "I should never have agreed to come here. I should have just stood my ground and said we were meant to go to Cambodia. We could have just hopped on a bus and been there in a day."

"So why didn't you?"

"Because I'm an idiot," I said, tapping my head with my knuckles. "I felt bad over getting us kicked out of the island place. So I just agreed. Thought it would make Anne happy. Now, look at me. The most miserable prick this side of Mount Everest."

"Not to worry," shrugged Viktor. "This place sucks anyway. Reminds me of the shit in India. Dirty, crowded, nothing works, and everyone is trying to screw you over. And, there are not that many girls around."

"What an utter mess," I relented with a sigh.

"Look," Viktor nodded sympathetically. "Maybe we should both just piss off to Thailand and have some fun, eh?"

"I'd be gone tomorrow," I confessed. "If it wasn't for Anne." Before Viktor could interrupt, I gave my reasoning. "Charles, her brother, would have my head if I just upped and left her here."

"Alright," shrugged Viktor. "Then call him up and tell him she's buggered off to a monastery and you want to leave. What's the worst that could happen?"

Viktor had a point. I didn't really give a damn about Anne anymore. I felt hurt and wanted answers, but knew I'd never get them. This was one of her ideas. She was old enough to make her own decisions, too. What was I meant to do, anyway? Wait around for a month while she got her spiritual kicks in a monastery? The mere thought of the idea made me angry. No, Viktor was right. This was also my holiday. I worked for it just as hard as Anne did. And I'd be damned if she was going to mess up my last few weeks.

***

The plan was simple. Go to Kathmandu and ask a bunch of monks if they knew one called Benji. Failing that, email Charles and tell him everything. Confess the works. Well, everything except sleeping with his sister. I suspected Anne never told him, nor was she going to either. So it was a safe thing to do. He always knew Anne was

170

a hippy wannabe, so the idea of her going off to some monastery shouldn't come as too big a shock.

Viktor had booked an express bus direct from Pokhara to Kathmandu. It got there in under six hours with no delays. It might have cost ten dollars more than Anne's local bus originally, but it included air-conditioning and they gave you a good buffet meal for lunch. A complete stranger from Putney in London on a rebel tour of India was now my best travel buddy. And aside from his constant talk of girls and immediate silence when around them, Viktor wasn't such a bad bloke.

"Namaste! Nice to see you back, Mr. J from the UK."

We'd only stayed one night, but the lady owner of the Garden House, Shanoli, remembered me. That was something Nepali people were very good at. Remembering people. Not so much their names, but faces and nationalities, yes.

"And this is a new friend you met when trekking?"

I nodded just to be polite. "Yea, this is Viktor. He's also from London."

"Ah, wonderful," beamed Shanoli with a wide smile. "And you'll also be going to volunteer at the monastery with your tall English lady friend?"

"Huh," I gasped. "You know Anne went to a monastery?"

"Of course," scowled Shanoli in jest. "She was here the other day with a monk."

"Really?"

"I know more about your friend than you do!" laughed Shanoli. She was a tiny lady, very Nepali looking. But her mannerisms and sarcasm were so western there was no problem talking with her. And it all made sense.

"Yea," I replied, feinting a laugh. "I just couldn't remember the name of the Monastery. Can't pronounce Nepali very well you know."

"Of course not," Shanoli quipped. "You're not Nepali. I am!"

Amid the laughter, I slipped in the one question we all wanted to know.

"So how do you pronounce the name of the Monastery."

"Easy," Shanoli replied. "T A N G U P A L A Monastery."

We had it. Simple as that. For once Nepal fell into place as easily as it continuously liked to fall apart around me. Taking some directions from the receptionist to avoid too much suspicion, we were even offered a local taxi man who could take us there. It looked like Anne was about to get a couple of unwanted and unexpected guests in the morning.

CHAPTER 21

THE CONFRONTATION

Monasteries in Nepal are big, yellow, and have lots of red trimming. They are also inconveniently perched at the top of big hills with no roads to drive up. Our taxi left us off at the bottom and we spent two hours both climbing up steps and asking every other person we met if this was the right way. Apparently, it was, no matter what direction we walked.

Making an educated guess it would always be up the hill, we eventually reached the eerily quiet large building compound.

"Do they like ... have an office or something?"

"Dunno," replied Viktor. "Never been to a monastery before."

"Me neither. Well, not a Nepali one anyway. They are really different from Thai ones."

"Well, it's big. And, yellow."

"Very yellow."

Every wall was painted a bright yellow, and every wooden door or window frame was painted a deep red. It was all new looking, too. It was built like a fort, complete with a surrounding outer wall and an inner courtyard. A far cry from your typical European old stone monasteries. Or the open-plan decorative Thai monasteries. There were also very few monks around. Which is also something I thought a monastery really should have.

"Maybe the monks have the day off?" I looked at Viktor to see if he was serious. He shrugged. "Well, do you have a better idea where everyone is?"

"There's one!" I ran up some concrete steps towards a lone monk in saffron robes. He was making his way across the open grass inner courtyard while reading from a small notebook.

"Hello, Namaste!" I greeted. He looked up with an emotionless face. Then did little else, but continued to walk. This was the first person I ever encountered, in all of Nepal, not to say Namaste.

"Namaste," I tried again. "We're looking for a volunteer you have working here."

The monk stared at me with big, sad eyes on a fairly dirty face. I thought back to my memories of anything to do with monks in Thailand. They were also pretty silent types. I then remembered monks from TV. Peace, praying, protesting, getting beaten up by foreign governments, and taking vows. Maybe he'd taken a vow of silence. A baby Thai monk, he was not. At least they smiled, occasionally.

"Tashi Delek," the Monk mumbled before sidestepping me and continuing with his walk.

"Friendly chap, eh?" remarked Viktor.

Leaving the lone monk to wander off, we explored around the inner courtyard for a while longer. Taking a chance, we peeked into any wooden door we'd find open. Some had shoes or, more often, flip-flops placed outside, but all were devoid of people. Moving upstairs, we finally found some life. Another relatively unfriendly monk walking between places and also not so happy to communicate with us.

"Maybe they really have taken a vow of silence?" offered Viktor.

"Yea, it's weird mate. I mean, aren't monks meant to be friendly and all that?"

"Like the laughing Buddha?"

"Yea."

"He was fat. These guys aren't. Maybe they're not eating enough?"

"There's one," I pointed over to a shaven-headed monk in his twenties coming out of a room. "Hey Namaste! Do you speak English?"

The monk turned towards us and, for once, didn't stay silent. Though he still didn't exactly smile, either.

"Tashi Delek," the monk said with a nod that might have been a bow, but I wasn't sure.

"Tashi Delek," I replied, nodding in the same manner and wondering if these words were the key to getting a monk to talk. "Namaste, do you speak English?"

"A little," replied the monk, pulling on the neck of his saffron robes. He said no more.

"We're looking for a volunteer you have here. Anne. Anne Roberts. Do you know where she is?"

"Volunteer Anne?"

"Yea, Anne. Tall girl, dark hair. Has an enormous jaw that twitches a bit ..."

"Yes," nodded the monk, pulling at his robes again. "Volunteer Ann helps with the children in Benji's school."

"Ah Benji," I nodded. "That's them. Do you know where we can find them?"

The monk spent a few seconds adjusting his robes yet again before telling us to follow him. Along the way, I tried making conversation, but it only resulted in nods along with a few yes's and no's or more robe adjusting. Nothing of any substance. This all led me to really question the belief that monks were super friendly. The only thing I found out was by asking what Tashi Delek meant.

"It is hello in Tibetan."

"So you speak Tibetan here?"

"Yes."

"Why is that then?"

"It is how we say hello."

"No, I mean why do you speak Tibetan."

"It is our way," replied the monk sombrely.

"But you are Nepali, right?"

Silence.

And again, the conversation ground to a stop. There was really more to Nepal than I ever thought before. So many layers of the unknown that were beginning to intrigue me. The monk led us around the upper floor to a doorway along a concrete corridor. There were some shoes outside, and I grinned when I saw Anne's gym shoes. Got her now.

"This is Benji's office," said the monk with another nod and robe adjustment before walking away slowly. "He will help."

"Thank you," I said as joyfully as I could. There was no reply. Perhaps Anne's personality was the reason they no longer wanted to communicate with foreigners.

"Do you want me to wait outside?" asked Viktor.

I thought about it for a minute. Then realised I wasn't sure what was about to happen. I was still angry, but not to the point of wanting to shout and roar like before. I just wanted to know what had happened to my laptop. I could also ask about what Anne was expecting me to do while she stayed here. Or what she thought about my plan to tell Charles. But in all honesty, I didn't give a damn anymore.

"No mate, it's alright. I can handle this. I'll give you a shout if I need anything. I just want to know if she has my laptop or not."

Reaching up to knock on the door, I realised the curtain in front of it prevented this from happening smoothly. When I tried to push the curtain back, I also managed to push the door wide open. I couldn't see anyone. It was a little dark inside.

"Hello?" I called out, trying to mask my voice a little.

No reply.

I went in.

The room was small with only one window and one light bulb lighting it up. There was no furniture except for a low corner table and several cushions on the ground. There was a curtain blocking off another door on the opposite wall, gently blowing in the breeze.

"Hello? Tashi Delek," I tried again.

There was a shuffling noise, and then the far curtain drew back, and a recognisable face appeared.

"Jonny?"

"Hello Anne."

"What are you doing here? And how did you …"

"Find you? Not hard."

Anne looked me up and down, then over my shoulder. Seeing nobody, she quickly settled into a more poised stance. "What do you want? And take off your shoes when you come inside."

I looked down and frowned. Apparently, shoe removal was a thing. I'd forgotten to remove them. One half of me wanted to remove them out of respect for the monastery, the other half didn't want to do anything Anne told me to do. I settled for ignoring her for now.

"Don't worry Anne, I'm not staying." Her shoulders relaxed a little along with her jawline. "I just want to know if you know where my laptop is?"

"Laptop?" she frowned. "What laptop?"

"My one, Anne," I said sarcastically. "The same one that was in my room the day before you left Pokhara, and the same one that went missing the next day."

Anne's face lit up in anger, and her jawline began that little twitching thing.

"What?"

"You went into my room without asking, didn't you?" I said, cutting her off.

"I was getting my stuff from inside. My stuff."

"Without asking me to go into my room?"

There was a brief silence, and I could see Anne struggling for an answer. "Why should I? It was my stuff. And, you were out drinking."

"It was my room. My locked room. Where my laptop went missing."

"Don't you accuse me of …" she paused. Her jawline twitched again. "I can't believe you would accuse me of something like that."

"I'm not accusing you of anything," I said sternly. "I just want to know if you saw it or know what happened to it?"

"No, I don't know anything about it."

The curtain behind Anne ruffled, and Benji the monk appeared. He looked at Anne and then at me. As per the norm, he didn't even say hello. Anne looked at him and shook her head in exaggerated distress. Benji the monk motioned for her to sit down. Almost looking like she was on the verge of tears, Anne crossed her legs and squatted down, followed by Benji the monk beside her near one of the cushions.

I repeated everything I knew from what the Pokhara guesthouse people had told me. If I let Anne get the upper hand, I'd lose. I needed to give her a reason to admit she'd taken it. Something to take the burden off her incoming victimisation plan.

"Look, we had a big bust-up at the Busy Bee," I said in a reasoning tone. "I don't care. I just want to know what happened to it?"

Mumbling something to Benji the monk, she nodded at him and then shook her head as if to confirm she would be okay in dealing with me.

"I didn't take your laptop, Jonny. And I …" she paused to look at Benji the monk again before turning back to me. "And I find it very tasteless of you to come in her accusing me of this."

"I didn't accuse you of anything, Anne," I re-confirmed. "I just want to know what happened to it. I mean, you were the only one that went into the room where it was last seen!"

I looked at Anne intensely. Her eyes were bloodshot and rigid. I'd seen the look before during many of our arguments. She believed in what she was saying. Glancing at Benji the monk, he turned to Anne. It was time to mention the witnesses.

"Someone took it, Anne. The guesthouse staff said you went in."

"So?" she snapped. "Did they say I walked out with your laptop?"

"They saw you go into my room when I wasn't there."

"It's Nepal Jonny. People go in and out of rooms here all the time."

"Did you even see it?"

"No, I didn't see any laptop. Why would I? I wasn't looking for it!"

The argument was lost. She wasn't budging, and I knew her well enough to know she would not confess to anything. In fairness, I also knew when she was telling the truth. And she was. My laptop was gone. And without outright accusing Anne of stealing it, she was right. I had no evidence to back anything up. The only thing that remained was an attempt at paranoia revenge.

"Fine, Anne," I said visibly, shrugging. "I'm not going to make a case out of it. The police in Pokhara have already opened a file about it."

Anne didn't react.

"Truth of the matter is, Anne, there's a GPS security system on the laptop. I can trace its whereabouts if it's stolen."

Anne didn't look impressed. But Benji the monk grabbed my attention. For the first time, I saw the emotion in his stare. His eyes flickered between Anne and me. I looked away in disbelief. It couldn't be. I looked at Benji the monk again. Dead in his eyes and did not falter. The moment had passed, though. He was back to his blank stare again.

"I don't care, Jonny," said Anne frankly. "If that's the case, then you should know where your laptop is?"

Stuck for words to back up my lie, I searched the back of my head for a suitable answer. But the only thing I could think about was that eye flicker from Benji the monk. The only other person to enter the room with Anne. And one of the reasons the old housekeeper lady in Pokhara didn't go into the room. She'd never question a man of faith. Neither would I. Until now.

"It's the weather," I finally blurted. "Lot's of clouds. Hard to get a lock on it. We'll know as soon as the person who stole it leaves it on for a while."

"Fine," said Anne, shaking her head in a non-caring way. "Then you'll have your answer. In the meantime, I think it's best you leave."

"Yea, me too," I said, looking down at her. "I'm going off to do my own thing."

"You do that."

"Probably leave Nepal."

"Fine."

"I'm just letting you know. You know, in case you need anything and I'm not around."

"I don't need anything from you, Jonny," she said with a forced snarl. "I've found my calling here."

"You're calling?" I gaffed.

"Yes," replied Anne, turning to Benji the monk. "The work we are doing here to help the children is what I was brought to Nepal for. I know that now."

"Eh? You came here because our visas ran out in Thailand."

"The world pushes us towards our destiny, Jonny. The sooner you accept that, the sooner you will lose all that hate inside you."

"Where are you getting all that crap from?"

Anne scowled at me and then extended a hand towards Benji the monk, and placed it over his. "I've learned a lot about finding my inner peace here thanks to Benji's teachings."

Benji the monk placed his other hand over Anne's and squeezed hers. Then Anne gazed at him for a moment that seemed too long. I knew that look. But again, my mind found it hard to accept. Nor comprehend. I felt my stomach instinctively tighten. Then, I let out an uncontrollable snort from my nose.

"My Gawd Anne," I said, wincing up my face. "You're not are you?"

"Damn you, Jonny," Anne snapped, pulling her hand back. "You're a sick and twisted little boy, aren't you?"

"Me? Sick and twisted? You're the one … "

Anne's jaw line went into hyper mode and her face filled with red rage. Benji the monk reached out and rubbed her back. She sighed and then bit her lower lip. Then the impossible happened.

"I don't hate you, Jonny, I love you." Anne, gnawed on her lower lip before continuing. "I love all creatures in the world. Good or bad. I wish your property returns to you. I don't hold value in any physical possessions any more."

A series of tears ran down Anne's flushed cheeks as Benji the monk urged her on with simple nods and mutterings so low I couldn't make them out.

"All I ask," she continued. "Is that you leave me be. Enjoy your world outside of here. I don't care about it. This is my calling for now. When I am ready, I will leave. Or stay."

What more could I say. The situation had completely gone belly up. No laptop. But instead, I had run into a situation I really wanted nothing to do with. I only hoped Anne hadn't completely lost the plot.

"Alright, Anne, have it your way," I said, looking at them both. "I won't bother you any more. But I am going to do the right thing and let your brother know where you are. I can't leave without telling Charles where his sister is."

"He already knows," Anne swallowed.

"You told him?"

"I told him I was going to spend the rest of the trip here volunteering and teaching the orphans how to speak English."

She was ahead of me again. "Okay, well I'll still send him a message, anyway."

No reaction.

"I'll tell him you're here, and I'm leaving. Just to be sure."

Silence.

There was little more to be said. I backed out of the little room with a glance at Anne and a final glare at Benji the monk. Anne never looked up. Benji did. Fleetingly.

CHAPTER 22

STARTING OVER AGAIN

There's a weird thing in Nepal. For a country that's so poor, the beer is very expensive. They grew most of the ingredients for beer and even brewed it. However, it was about the same price as a pint back home. These things seemed to buzz around my head the more I tried to figure Nepal out. But the more I tried, the more I found it contradictory. It didn't matter tonight. Viktor was kindly buying. He'd heard the whole conversation with Anne and figured it was worthy of being noted as the biggest screw job he'd ever come across in real life.

"I'll never look at a monk the same way again," he said, bringing over another big bottle of Nepal Ice from the guesthouse restaurant's fridge. "I wonder if it happens often?"

"What? That a monk can shag or the stealing thing?"

"Does it matter, mate? They're both pretty high in the religious order of things not to do."

"Yea, I guess. But isn't Buddhism a way of life and not a religion?"

"Don't look at me. I'm clueless. I didn't even know what to do the first time I went into a Hindu temple in India."

"Same thing you do back home?"

"No, I didn't do it there either."

It was still early, and we were already well on our way to drowning the day's events. I'd sent Charles an email before joining Viktor for a night out in Thamel. I kept the email to a minimum. An email felt better than a message.

Hi Charles,

Got your last message. Sorry didn't reply, internet over here sucks.

Anyway, I think Anne sent you a message already about volunteering at the monastery? What do you think about it?

To be really honest with you, we haven't been hitting it off. And I don't really want to hang around this place for the next three weeks waiting for Anne to finish up finding peace and love and all that.

I hope you're okay with that?

Jonny.

I then followed up with an FB message.

Charles, sent you an email.

The thing with an FB message was I could see when he'd read it. And could then gauge if there was going to be a fallout or not.

I had no idea what Anne had said to Charles in her own messages, so I played it simple. My main thing was to get a blessing from him saying it was alright to leave her to her own devices. The plan was to wait a few days for a reply and, in the meantime, figure out what to do next. Which, according to Viktor, had already been decided.

"You're going back to Thailand. And, I'm going too," he smiled.

"Huh?" I replied. "Thailand?"

"I mean, you told that ex of yours you were leaving, right? And, you already said you preferred it over in Thailand, right? So what's stopping you?"

I shrugged, and Viktor continued on with the new plan. "Anyway Jonny, like I said before. I've had enough of this place, too. I need to get out of all this, mate. Nepal is too much like India for me. That's my parents' thing. Me, I want to chill out and relax. So, Whaddaya say?"

The answer should have been an immediate yes get me the hell out of here. But something strange kept nagging at me. At first, I thought it was the guilt about leaving Anne behind. Then I moved on to the thought of not having done anything much in Nepal. Then I thought about the trek I never went on, and the one solitary trip I did on a motorbike and saw the Annapurna mountains. For all its dirt, mishaps, terrible food, lack of communication, random electricity, and woeful internet, something about Nepal was grabbing at me. Telling me something I couldn't quite translate into any sense. I gave Viktor a dull excuse to buy some time to figure it all out.

"The tickets? My return date is not for another three weeks?"

"So?" shrugged Viktor. "I've not bought any yet. But today I asked Shanoli about Nepal Air's tickets and she said they fly to Bangkok twice a week. And you can change your dates with them no hassle."

"Really?"

"Yea, mate, we can go in two days if we want. Just like you guys arrived on short notice. It's Nepal. It's not like booking a ticket from London to Paris tomorrow. Booking online and all that shit. Just pay 'em cash here and off you go."

I laughed. Another plus for stepping back in time into Nepal. Viktor was right. I remembered the booking lady in Bangkok saying we could change our dates whenever we wanted. And the more Viktor kept selling me the idea of just getting up and leaving, the more I liked it.

"Bluewater," continued Viktor. "White beaches, cocktails and soooooo many hot girls running around. It's time to live a little Jonny. Screw all this crap, let's go party on an island!"

I raised my glass, and we toasted the deal. A return to Thailand and a goodbye to the bad times. It was time for a holiday reboot.

"You're leaving?"

It was the guesthouse owner, Shanoli. She wasn't upset we were leaving so soon. Just curious. We invited her over and confessed all. Shanoli wasn't at all surprised at either the laptop situation or if indeed Benji the monk and Anne were sleeping together. She took in her stride and was more interested in listening to our plans in Thailand. The conversation was enlightening, to say the least.

The three of us drank well into the evening. We laughed and made jokes about my gaffs in Thailand and Nepal. Shanoli gave great gasps of exaggerated shock before breaking out into a huge laugh as if life was made for not being taken too seriously.

"Stupid monks," she said, grinning. "I don't like them. They always up to something."

I nervously toasted the notion. Still not sure it was the right thing to do or even think. Viktor had no issues with it. Instead, he and Shanoli hit it off on the subject of how to talk to women. It was a strange night. A completely different side to Nepal I'd never experienced before. Maybe it was just Shanoli. Maybe it was the beer. No, it was Shanoli alright. She seemed quite different from all the other Nepali I'd met so far. She was normal. She talked to us like people and not customers. I liked the feeling. Best of all, she agreed that it was time for a holiday reboot. But first, we needed to see the real Kathmandu with her in the morning. She offered to take us to Durbar Square. The very centre of an ancient kingdom, I knew nothing, rather embarrasingly, about.

We ate breakfast and walked out of the guesthouse with Shanoli onto the dusty streets of Kathmandu. She led us across some winding paths and down red-bricked alleys that I never knew existed before.

"You don't want to stay in Thamel to see Kathmandu," beamed Shanoli. "Thamel is full of stupid people!"

Viktor laughed at Shanoli's bluntness. "You are certainly a tough lady!"

"I am Nepali lady," retorted Shanoli as she brought us past a white dome in the middle of a square. "Stupid old men run our country. If you don't shout, they don't listen."

With that, we both fell silent. I wasn't sure if Shanoli was bashing men in general, her government, or just the men in her government. Either way, I figured it was best not to ask.

"This is Kathesimbhu Stupa," Shanoli said, pointing up an alley to another, larger white stupa.

I looked at the impressive structure as we walked closer. It had a tall golden spire that sat above a solid bright white dome. With only a drop of imagination, it looked a little like an inverted ice cream cone. Only when I thought about it like that, I felt a little strange.

Shanoli explained it was a Newari stupa. The Newari were apparently the first people to create Kathmandu. There was a legend about another Stupa that this one is a copy of that rose up out of a valley filled with water when Kathmandu was formed. The Newari people also had their own religion, which was a blend of Hinduism and Buddhism.

All around the stupa were stone markers known as chaitya, statues of deities, and markings in the stone slabs. Shanoli continued to explain things to us as we continued on walking, but I was having a hard time taking it all in. I'd thought Nepal was Buddhist, but the majority are apparently Hindu, yet the founders are Newari, only they are not the founders of Nepal, just Kathmandu. The founder of Nepal was actually another king that invaded them. On top of all that, Buddhism was more than just a cross-legged guy talking about peace called The Buddha. He also has a name, Siddhartha. Apparently, he was also only one of many buddhas. I don't remember any of this being mentioned back in school, nor did Anne mention any of this during her quest for monasteries and monks. All I'd ever been told about Nepal was that's where Mount Everest was. In truth, Nepal was far more complex than just being home to the world's tallest mountain.

We continued walking down the narrow streets that soon turned from tarmac to concrete, to stone slabs, to cobblestone. It was as if the further we got from Thamel, the further back in time we went. Even Viktor seemed a little impressed by all this. When he mentioned something about a Hindu god in India, of which there are thousands, Shanoli reminded him he was in Nepal now, and this is where the Hindu gods came to rest.

Before we even entered Durbar Square, Shanoli was already talking about it. A place where the Newari kings once lived and created Kathmandu, the city. But before I knew we were even inside the square, Shanoli shouted at us to hide!

"Over here, quick," she hushed as she led us through an archway to the left. "I don't want you paying for this. They take your money and line their pockets and never repair anything!"

We stood behind the stone arch peeping out. I could just about make out two tourists standing by a little cabin along the road we'd been on, arguing with a man in uniform. It didn't take long before they were reaching for their wallets.

"I don't mind paying," offered Viktor, who looked a little worried about our criminal endeavour.

"No," scolded Shanoli, "This is the only city square in the entire world where they force you, tourists, to pay. Don't do that. They don't repair this place, they just eat the money."

I looked at Viktor and signalled not to make an issue out of it. This was Shanoli's city, not ours. If we get caught, we'll just pay whatever the rate is and say sorry we never noticed that little cabin. With that, she led us around a corner and out another arch. This is when my mind fell into another world.

I stood there gazing out at what I can only describe as a cityscape that a fantasy movie director could create. Tall red brick, with part-whitewashed walls, and dark wood temples with multiple tiered roofs stood all around us. I'd never seen anything like it before.

Even Viktor gave an appreciative nod. "Nice. I guess it's old?"

"Of course it's old," admonished Shanoli in jest. "This is the real Nepal, thousands of years old.

The half dozen or so buildings in front of us could have formed a magnificent mystical painting. Such brilliant reds, naturally toned woods, mesmerising tiered roofs that reached up to a brilliant blue sky. Pigeons that flocked around their bases flew up in great numbers as people walked by on the way to a temple to bless themselves. Unlike what I was used to, these blessings took place at the bottom or outside of a temple instead of inside. Some lit incense that sent wafts of scented smoke into the air, others left bright orange flowers or lit candles. It was as if we'd simply walked into a different time as opposed to a place where time stood still. This was all very much alive in the present.

From across the street, a figure approached us like something out of a Star Wars movie. A tall man with a staff and a painted face on a mission. He had long grey hair which highlighted the bright yellow and red paint that covered a quarter of each part of the top part of his face. As he came closer, I noticed that he only wore a loincloth and cape. The rest of his exposed body was covered in grey ash.

"This is a Sadhu," explained Shanoli, "A holy man. He wants money if you take his photo."

For the first time on my trip, I actually wanted a photo. I took my phone out and began taking photos as if looking to take proof that a place like this existed.

"20 rupees only!" snapped Shanoli, bringing me back to reality.

I handed a crumpled note to the Sadhu who placed it in a metal bowl without a word. I kept taking photos and uploading them to Instagram as if I'd just discovered Shangri-La.

"Over here," beckoned Shanoli with a big smile. "You are enjoying, huh?"

I nodded in innocence while Viktor shrugged and mentioned a Hindu gods statue he recognised at one temple. I wondered if he had seen something like this in India? For the first time, that I recalled, Viktor gave a head wobble and said nothing.

Shanoli smiled widely, "Do want to see the Living Goddess?"

"Huh?" I replied quizzically. "What do you mean?"

"The Kumari," answered Shanoli. "She is the Living Goddess of Kathmandu and the Newari. She lives over here."

We walked through the wide-open stone paths of Durbar Square, past tall mythical towers that were each dedicated to different gods. High steps led up to most of the temples, while others lay behind carved wooden doors. It was all so mesmerising. Why had I never seen all this before?

Shanoli led us to the Kumari's house. An open wooden courtyard. Apparently, the Living Goddess appears, randomly, at a window about two floors up. We waited a while but she never appeared. I didn't know if I was disappointed, or if the strange feeling of longing to know more abated it all.

I could have spent the day in Durbar Square and was even more taken back when Shanoli said there were even more beautiful squares than this in nearby cities. I wasn't so much ashamed that I'd never really taken the time to learn about Nepal. I was, after all, not expecting to visit the country. I was simply feeling a little dumbfounded that I never knew such a place existed in the first place.

On our walk back to the guest house, Shanoli joked with us about how so many people visit Nepal to see mountains or go trekking but they never see the real Nepal. I took that as a saving grace for my own visit.

We ate dinner together at the guest house on what was to be our last night. Somehow, Shanoli had instilled in me the satisfaction about visiting places in Nepal I never knew about before. I felt like I'd only seen the tip of an iceberg and yet already my time in the country was up. Tomorrow would be so different, but also so familiar.

***

What was once a mass of heaving humanity in Bangkok seemed like civilization to me now. There were crowds moving everywhere, but unlike in Nepal, everyone was moving with purpose in Thailand's capital. The efficiency compared to Nepal was mind-blowing.

We took a train from the airport into downtown Bangkok. It was faster, easier, and more comfortable than the bus. Then we hopped on a sky train for a short ride to a travel agent in Silom. Just before leaving Nepal, we figured out we didn't even need to stay in Bangkok if we arrived at lunchtime. Which we did. If all went to plan, we would be taking an overnight bus straight to the ferry port and then over to Haad Rin Beach. It was all so easy compared to Nepal. We retreated to a coffee shop to wait for the bus.

"I'd nearly forgotten what beautiful girls look like," Viktor joked, looking out the window. "I can't believe they cover up so much in Nepal and India. It's just not right."

He had a point. Even after a few weeks in Nepal, I couldn't help but stare at a few Thai girls walking by on the street. Beside them on the congested road, people still stayed in the same lanes. And the traffic lights worked. Everything that was once hot, humid, and dirty was now fresh, clean, and simply worked. It was a strange feeling.

We just sat there for a while and stared out at Bangkok's living show. This time, Thailand felt very different, and I felt prepared for it.

Before leaving Nepal, I'd also sent Matt and Jeff from the Pink Fish a message asking if it was okay, and safe, to come back. They wrote back, wondering what the problem was? They'd either forgotten about my run-in with the law there or else had forgotten who the hell I was. It didn't matter; we were going anyway. If they didn't want us, there was sure to be another beach nearby. All I wanted was to chill back and forget about the past few weeks. This was made all the better as Charles had also replied to my email about leaving Anne in Nepal.

Hi Jonny,
Yea, I got a message from Anne. She mentioned you guys were not doing so well. Truth be told, I didn't think you'd make it this far with her LOL.
Anne's a big girl now, so don't worry about it. I know where she is, so it's fine.
It's pissing cats n dogs down over here so I'm jealous as hell.

Charles.

I had no more obligations. Charles was cool with me leaving Anne. Anne didn't care. And, if I gave a crap, I'd still be raging about everything. But I wasn't. I was fairly relaxed and looking forward to a beach, a swim, and a nice long massage after one of those nice Thai Green curries.

Even the overnight bus turned up on time. Every time something 'just worked' I'd compare it to the disaster of Nepal. Heck, even the toilet on the bus worked. I couldn't even remember any toilet, fully working in Nepal. Thailand was easy. Which was strange because when I'd first arrived, it was bloody hard. At least the hassles were. Compared to Nepal, the Thai touts were amateurs.

I put my earphones in to drown out the noise of a bus full of backpackers with no intention of sleeping for the night. Staring out at a city filled with lights, we took off at speed with cool air flowing down around us from the air conditioning. Thoughts of Anne drifted away. The dirty streets of Nepal became faded shadows of the past. I thought only briefly about the mountains, the caring old housekeeper lady, and the joy Shanoli's humour had brought us on our last few days. They were the good things to remember. I did briefly think about my broken tooth. I'd heard there were good dentists in Thailand, so I made a mental note. With thoughts about the beach, the sea, and falling asleep under the warm sun, I nodded off.

"Jonny! Wake up, mate!" Viktor was nudging me with his elbow. "We're here I think."

Outside, the landscape had changed. Gone were the dark shadows of Bangkok's sparkling high-rise buildings and rushing people. There was no sign of Nepal's low rise crumbling buildings and sways of people crowding the streets. Beside me was the first inkling of paradise in the form of the aqua blue sea and the bright yellow sands of Thailand's southern coast. In under an hour, we were even further into paradise lined with tall palms. A short ferry ride and I was back on Haad Rin beach. It was easier this time. I knew the way. I even remembered a few words of Thai to shoo away the touts. Viktor stuck close to me and I felt confident in leading my friend with no errors to the Pink Fish.

"Jonny!" the pink t-shirts were unforgettable. Matt and Jeff were still running the place and looking more like beach bums every day. "What's up, man? Where have you been all this time?"

"I need a beer to tell you about that one," I gleamed.

"Ha ha, no worries," Matt said, pulling a can of Singha Thai beer out from a foam icebox he was carrying. "I got you a real nice cottage up at the end of the beach. Away from the noise and not so far from the party, eh!"

"Cool, sounds good."

"Are we sharing?" asked Viktor.

I looked at him and shook my head in jest, "I sincerely hope not after listening to you snore on the bus all night."

In the end, Viktor got a cottage next to mine. He was also thrilled at seeing the Pink Fish menu placed on his bedside table. Aside from a room service of drinks, meals, and a host of activities from snorkelling to scuba diving, it also included sports massages, relaxation massages, and about five other variations of massage. The Pink Fish had moved up in the world thanks to peak season, plus Matt and Jeff's attempts at getting more people to stay. Or, in my case, getting people to return and stay longer. They'd taken over the local cottages, and were doubling up on profits because of it.

"This place is unreal." Viktor stood in the doorway to my cottage with the massage menu in his hand. "I just ate a coconut and crab soupy thing for about two quid!"

"Yea, tasty too," I said, relaxing back on my bed. I had made it a priority to soak up every relaxing moment I could since coming back. No more stress, no more crap. Time to enjoy life and not think about returning to rainy England for three more weeks.

"Have you done a scuba dive Jonny?"

"No never. It's an idea though."

"Think we can find some girls to go out with us?"

"Ha ha, is that all you think about, Viktor?"

"What you don't?"

"Tell you what. Let's chill out for a while, then head up to the bar this evening and see who's staying here. Have a few drinks and enjoy it. I'm sure you'll meet some girls there."

"Excellent! Think I might get one of those massages first. Sounds awesome. Only a fiver!"

"Enjoy it mate, enjoy."

With the door left open, I watched the bright blue sea roll up to the white, sandy island shore. A ceiling fan whirred above me, sending a cool breeze over my body as I stretched away the past few weeks. Everything was feeling good. So good, I just let myself lie there and doze off for the afternoon. Taking an odd dip in the sea to cool down now and then. I couldn't have asked for more. But it came anyway.

On the way back from one of my cooling swims, I met a bunch of Australian surfer types from a nearby cottage. They were catching afternoon waves and lapping in Thailand at its finest. I joined them and had my first surfing lesson with a girl called Julie from their group. Even though I could do no more than kneel on the board, no one cared. We drank cocktails as the sun came down and discovered we all liked the idea of doing a scuba dive together sometime over the next week. It all happens as simply as that in Thailand.

The only thing I wondered about was how Viktor was going to cope with this newfound freedom. By eight that first night, he was already inebriated to the point of not being able to order another drink by himself, let alone getting back to his cottage under his own steam. That duty fell to me.

"Jonnnny ..." he slurred. "It bloody fantastic here."

"Yea, I know Viktor. Can you try lifting your feet a little higher over the sand?"

"It's soooo beautiful. It'ssss Paradisssse."

"Yep."

"Paradise Jonny!"

"Yep."

"An' my parents wanted me to stay in INDIA. I shur've just come 'ere."

"Yep. Nearly there now."

"I don't care. I'll sleep here under the stars mate."

"Do that tomorrow, mate. The mosquitos will get you if you sleep on the beach. You can sleep outside tomorrow okay."

"Yea mate, tomurrrrrow."

Only two more trip-ups and face firsts into the sand and finally I managed to get Viktor back to his cottage. But not before Julie came out from the cottage beside his and Viktor spotted her.

"Hey Jonny," beamed Viktor. "There's that cute Ozy girl."

I waved at Julie and thankfully she saw the state Viktor was in and waved back with a smile. Viktor fell onto his bed and briefly opened his eyes as I turned to leave. "Hey Jonnny."

"What mate?"

"I … I just want to say thanks, mate."

"Sure no problem."

"No, I mean thankssss. Thanks for showing me this place. It's really awesommme."

"No worries Viktor. Sleep it off and tomorrow we start the same thing all over again."

"Awesommme," like some giant smiling baby, Viktor closed his eyes with a wide grin. "And I know what I want in the morning."

"What's that then?"

"A massaaaage."

"Goodnight Viktor," I laughed, closing the door. Then I wondered for a moment what Viktor had been doing all afternoon. Turns out, according to Julie, who'd heard it from Matt and Jeff, Viktor was now the Pink Fish's number one massage client. And their best tipper.

CHAPTER 23

A BETTER KIND OF PARTY

Over the next two weeks on Haad Rin beach, I managed to forget about the previous two months' troubles. I got up between nine and ten in the morning with no obligation to do anything other than to enjoy life. My morning wash was a swim in the sea followed by a rinse off in the small shower behind the Pink Fish bar. Then, waiting at my regular table would be my breakfast. I'd started with buttery pancakes and crispy bacon during my first few days, but was now moving on to mixed fruit salads sprinkled with coconut shavings with toast topped with a drizzle of honey. My way of staying healthy. Life felt good at last. Adding to this was being a part of Viktor's various antics as he figured out his own way through life.

"Gawwwwd, my head hurts …" Viktor emerged from his morning of sleeping off the night before. "I need to change from those tequila shots, I think."

"I'm not sure it's even real tequila, mate. Tastes more like local firewater."

"That would explain a lot." he grimaced against the sun as he put on a pair of dark designer sunglasses. "What's up today? We going out or chilling on the beach?"

"Are you up for a dive in an hour or two?"

"I'll let you know after brekkie."

I rarely stayed up past two in the morning, but Viktor could easily go all night drinking and smoking. He normally woke up around midday and then filled me in on his escapades the night before. I'd laugh at his tales of chatting up various girls, but took most of it with a grain of salt. Though giving him some credit, Viktor had come a long way out of his shell since arriving. These days, he wouldn't sit in silence when we joined a group at the beach. He still needed a few beers to really get going, though. A potential problem in all this was that he'd discovered some "special" massages from a nearby place after ordering a regular massage one afternoon. I remembered my accidental massage in Bangkok when I'd arrived, so didn't think it proper to say anything about it. He was enjoying himself and supporting the local economy. His words, not mine.

As for me, I was content with my blossoming friendship with Julie, the surfer from Australia. We'd got on well since meeting on my first day back on the island. She was the fifth one out in a group of two couples, so had no problem wanting to meet others. Julie even thought Viktor was funny in the way he suddenly fell silent around girls and had been the main person encouraging him to come out of his shell. Most of this happened during our scuba diving in the afternoons. We all chipped in and rented equipment from a local dive centre. Two of Julie's friends were dive masters, so we learned the ropes from them. Nothing serious, but a lot of fun. We'd then chill on the beach for the afternoon.

"I'm dreaming of Julie on a white beach," sang Viktor to the tune of White Christmas.

"Shut up."

"What? You still haven't made the moves on her then?"

"I told you it's not like that. We're just …"

"Friends," he laughed. "Yea, yea, so you keep saying. Listen, mate, you're out of here soon. You really need to get working on this before you leave."

"Actually Julie's leaving in two days."

"What? Why?"

"Just time to move on. I mean, they've been here for a few weeks, so I guess they want to see some more of Thailand."

"Bummer mate."

What I didn't tell Viktor is that things with Julie got a bit more interesting over a week ago. It was after a great day of diving and a mini party over on another beach. I elected to walk her home since one of the couples had promised to carry Viktor back if need be. Julie was your average sporty outdoors type of girl. Tough to get to know unless you could keep up with her. But that day I'd impressed her by spotting a barracuda lurking in a beautiful display of colourful coral. Only its head was visible and as I swam near, it came out to warn me off without fear. I beckoned Julie over to have a look and it performed a wonderful show of teeth before backing into its coral home to eye us up from relative safety. Thailand's rich ocean was filled with kaleidoscopic life that made the word tropical come alive in my heart. It was our topic of conversation on the walk back. And again as we sat together outside on the steps to her cottage alone, staring out into the dark sea and listening to the waves come in.

"It's been really amazing to team up with you guys for scuba since arriving," I said in all honesty.

"Yea, it's been good over here too," she replied, flicking back her long, dark blond fringe. "I was really feeling like a fifth wheel with all those couples around."

"You're nobody's fifth wheel." I cringed at my corniness. And so did Julie. "Seriously though, thanks for the surfing lessons, too. A week ago, I couldn't even sit on a board. Now I can …"

"Get to one knee!" she laughed.

"Yea, yea, well thanks for helping me get that far."

"No probs," Julie's eyes sparkled, and I got the sense she wanted me to kiss her.

I smiled back as I gently looked at her lips and moved closer. A mere few inches away, and I could feel her warmth.

"Jonny …" she whispered.

I felt my heart pound.

"I've a boyfriend."

My eyes closed and my face winced as my heart returned to normal. I pulled back and Julie was still smiling, but looking a little sad. At least I thought so.

"He's back home in Darwin, at work," she said, almost like a confession. "We've been together two years."

"It's cool," I lied and sat up straight. "I can handle that."

She laughed, and we both went through that little awkwardness of not knowing what to say next. Instead, I made some remark about wondering if Viktor had passed out on her mates yet or not. And that was the evening. It was all good, though. Once I might have been disappointed. But I'd met a new friend who liked me for me. So for the first time in my life, I felt good about a relationship that never happened. We bid each other goodnight with a kiss on the cheek.

Since then we've got on famously. There were no more hang-ups or uncertainties. Julie was suddenly like one of my best mates. Once everything was out in the open, there was no more pretence. We made plans for our last few days in paradise. One more dive, and a big half-moon party.

***

And what a half-moon party it was. Music thumped into the night as bonfires on Haad Rin Beach rose into the darkness. We danced to the beat of Euro tech music and the occasional break out of eighties rock music. There was no need for smokes, blue indigo or buckets of rum. We were high on the feeling of life.

Viktor was doing well, too. He had not had a drink all day and only one joint. This was all Julie's influence. She had a sit-down talk with him about learning to relax more and drink less. It seemed to have worked. He even drew up the courage to dance with one girl while sober. I'd miss all this. In two days, I'd be leaving too.

"Jonny," Julie said as the music died down. "Come to Australia next year."

"To do what?" I said as we collapsed back into the night sand.

"Visit me, of course," laughed Julie.

"Yea, and I'll say hi to your boyfriend too at the same time, eh?" Julie glanced tersely at me.

"Just kidding," I confessed. "It would be cool to meet up with both of you over there."

Again there was some awkwardness and I couldn't help feel that Julie wanted to say something else. Again, I wasn't going to push anything. I was just enjoying her company and my last night. I walked Julie back one last time to her cottage. But we said nothing along the way. She turned at the doorway and put a hand on my shoulder. Then she pressed her lips onto mine and let them linger for a moment.

"Thanks, Jonny," she said, pulling back. "Thanks for a wonderful time here."

I smiled back and my heart swelled with something I don't think I've ever felt before. What an idiot I was. I should have grabbed her and kissed her back. Told her we should go with the flow of our feelings. Then again, maybe my heart swelled because I didn't. Instead of being brash, I stood there as she said goodnight and gently closed the door.

I sat outside my cottage by myself and listened to the waves. One half of me wanted to knock on Julie's door. The other half told me to be happy with what I'd just experienced. I met someone who genuinely liked me. It felt good.

"What's with the early night, mate?" Viktor was on his way back to his own cottage when he spotted me sitting on the porch and came over.

"Nothing, just enjoying the night here, that's all."

"No, go with Julie, then I take it?"

"No. No, go. And, it's just fine."

"Hard luck mate."

"Cheers. I'm good though."

"Maybe we'll have better luck in Bangkok in a few days."

"Huh? We?"

"Yea? I'm hardly going to let you piss off back to England without having a big send-off in the city of sin."

"You're coming to Bangkok?"

"'course I am mate," Viktor grinned. "I want to check out the place myself, you know. I heard the girls are dead easy up there. Dead easy."

"Is that all you think about?"

"No, sometimes I think it's about time to get married too."

"Piss off!"

Viktor laughed and then pulled out a small joint. Lit it up and handed it over to me. I thought about it, then smiled, shook my head and handed it back to him.

"Nah," smiled Viktor as he inhaled. "It's time to blow this place, anyway. Won't be the same without you here. So I figure we'll take you up to Bangkok. Send you off with a bang. And then, I'll try checking out this Chiang Mai place you told me about before pissing off back home myself."

"Yea? Back to England? What are you going to do there?"

"Go to work," Viktor paused, then looked down at the sand before continuing. "Work. Work with my father and brother in our Estate Agent business I guess."

"What? You're going to be an estate agent?"

"Yea," Viktor said, blowing out a long plume of smoke. "My obligation to the family an' all that. Bloody joke. But that's what we do in Putney, you know."

I couldn't imagine Viktor selling real estate. Then again, I had no idea what I'd be doing in a week either. I was flat broke. Something told me I'd be working in Sainsbury's as a bag boy. So Viktor's lot in life back home seemed quite a bit higher up the ladder than mine. Our days living in tropical paradise were indeed numbered. Maybe that's what made them feel so good.

CHAPTER 24

A RETURN TO THE BIG CITY

Bangkok was as hot and concrete as it always was. We'd been loaded off the bus and surrounded by touts immediately. For the second time, I was hoping the original tout when I'd first arrived would make a reappearance. But there was no sign of him. So I carried my own bag and shooed away the replacement touts. We ended up back at the same guesthouse again, too. It's always easier to return to a place you know the lay of the land with. Only this time Viktor had suggested we get a private twin en-suite room, as it was my last couple of nights on holiday. A dorm room didn't seem so appealing and Viktor offered to pay, so I had no objections.

I sent Charles a note on messenger letting him know how things were.

Then I sent Anne a very brief one.

I'm back in Bangkok staying at the same place as before. I'm flying out on Thursday, no change in my ticket.
Just letting you know.

I was tempted to send a screenshot to Charles. But as he had said, Anne was big enough to look after herself. If she didn't show up for the plane, so be it. Should I be worried? I'd be lying if I said no. But only in the sense that Charles and her family might blame me for ditching her in Nepal. So I sent Charles another message just to confirm.

> *BTW I sent Anne a message letting her know I was leaving on the 28th, the same day as her ticket too.*
> *She's not been in contact with me at all.*
> *I hope she'll let you know if she's coming back on that date, too.*

Then I saw the read note. Then, the worst fear for anyone sending 'just a message' on messenger. He called.

"Hey Jonny!" Charles' chiseled face filled my phone's screen.

"Hey Charles, good to see you!"

"I just read your note about Anne," he started. "Look, she's a rebel. Always has been, always will be."

I nodded and kept my mouth shut for once.

"I spoke to mum and dad," he paused and scratched at his chin. "To be honest, they are freaking out a bit that she's not with you."

I raised my eyebrows and waited for some sort of 'rescue' plea. But it didn't come.

"She's at a monastery," Charles continued. "It could be worse, it could be some sort of weird cult thing she ended up at."

I could see Charles was worried, but I also had to distance myself from Anne's antics. So, I just nodded in agreement. Charles was a protective big brother, but he also knew his sister was well able to look after herself. Well, make up her own mind about things.

"Oh wait," exclaimed Charles, looking startled. "I just saw her come online now. Let me go call her, okay?"

"Sure mate, no worries."

"Listen, have a great time," waved Charles as I saw him hurriedly swiping across the screen, "You look like a beach bum!"

"Thanks buddy!"

"See you soon".

"Bye Charles."

And that was it. I was off the hook with Anne.

"Hey, Jonny mate?"

Distracted by Viktor coming into the café, I swiped messenger off. "What's up?"

Viktor looked a little awkward. "You know those massage places on every corner here?"

"Emm, yea?"

"Well, like, are all the massage places, … you know. Happy places?"

"Jeez, Viktor," I groaned with a cheesy grin. "What's up with you man?! Come on it's Bangkok. I'm leaving soon. Let's wash up and go out to some real bar and leave all that happy ending crap behind."

Viktor paused in thought. His big, mischievous smile dropped a little in the process.

"Meh, you've got a good point," he mused. "I'll catch up with Lady Big Heart's parlour when you've gone."

I wasn't sure if Viktor was joking or not. I didn't care. He laughed at the idea, and it was contagious. Apart from the European girl next to me in the café, who gave us both a disgusted look before shuffling over in her seat to get some distance.

"It's him, not me." I grinned in extroverted confidence.

Silence.

She continued staring at her phone, typing away.

No problem.

We left.

The streets of Bangkok were teeming with people, as always. I realised now there was more to Bangkok than just temples. In fact, the best places in Bangkok were the side streets. Here you'd find all manner of people and places. From humble street cafes selling all types of bowls of chopped up noodle soup to deep-fried chicken parts to iced coffee vendors. Air conditioning units dripped down on you from high above unless you walked closer to the stores. And then when you did, you had to manage to avoid all the people shuffling to do the same.

Walking on the roads meant death by taxi or random motorcyclist speeding by. Not to mention the sun's heat that was exposed on every road. All this and in nearly every section of Bangkok city, there was a massage parlour. The closer you got to touristy bars, the more appeared. Outside, each would be a small group of four or five girls or young men with little laminated massage menus and matching uniforms. When they'd see you coming, they pretended not to notice. Then, as you walked by, one of them would make the effort to stand up and thrust out a menu or pamphlet in front of you.

"Massaaaage sir, you wan?" they would all drone.

Nevermore, never less. Always, that long extended 'Massaaaage'. The girls rarely say more until you look at them. Then they lock their eyes onto yours with military precision before unleashing pretty smiles. The type of smile you only ever see in a nightclub after a few drinks and making as much contact as possible with a girl you're attracted to. You knew the look immediately if she reciprocated. It says to every hormone in your body I like you, I want you. To avoid all this happening in Bangkok, the solution was simple. Don't make eye contact with anyone outside massage parlours. They lose interest in a heartbeat. Yes, once this would have interested me. But now, I saw it as a money catcher. I saw it as a different obsession. I saw it as something I didn't have an interest in anymore.

Even Viktor had learned this trick. He did what I did. He looked from a distance as any red-blooded single guy would do. If there was a pretty girl, fine. If not, fine. Either way, we never looked at anyone as we passed by. Well, we did occasionally. But I found it more entertaining to watch Viktor pretend he wasn't looking, then catch him out when he was obvious about it. The biggest shock came when he looked at one of the male masseurs who offered a massage. Who then made direct eye contact with Viktor and smiled seductively at him. Viktor looked petrified. As such, the lesson was never to look anyone in the eye outside a Thai massage parlour unless you were really planning a massage.

Back at the guesthouse, we showered and later on ate a celebratory dinner in Chinatown consisting of huge Thai river prawns, Pad Thai noodles all washed down with a cold beer. It was then onto one of the oddities of Bangkok, something called a Milk Bar. And yes, sure enough inside they sold milk and thick toast. Kind of like a bar for babies. Except it was full of normal adults inside, eating big slices of flavoured toast and giant glasses of milk. One of the quirky things I was quickly beginning to like about Bangkok.

"Girlllls, you wannnn?"

A tout of some kind forced a little black business card into our hands as we left the milk bar. It was a drinking voucher for a Chinatown go-go bar. One free drink for every two drinks you ordered. An image of a scantily clad Thai girl took up half the card with the words 'May your dreams cum true,' written in pink over her.

"Sounds good?" beamed Viktor.

"Every tourist bar in Bangkok sounds like this. What they don't tell you is that the first drink costs as much as three normal ones." I walked up into the sky train ticket area. "What we need is a place that won't scam us."

"Sukhumvit is where everyone says to go."

"Okay then, let's go!"

Getting around Bangkok was easy on the sky train. And within a few stops, we were at Sukhumvit. Bangkok's expat and touristy zone. By now, the night cafes were in full swing and every inch of pavement was taken up with street vendors and their assorted tables. The cooler nighttime air made it all the more tolerable and brought out the crowds. We took a turn down one side street to look at some craft vendors, but were quickly surrounded by a street of bars with all manner of neon lights flashing outside. Touts handed out a mix of leaflets. Some offered drinks, others live girls. A few offered male dancing, but all offered a similar type of experience. We took the plunge and went into the first bar, which didn't look as sleazy as the others.

The drinks were reasonably priced and the music loud. We took a table by a wall with a giant photograph of Marilyn Monroe hanging above us.

"You waaaan special drink?"

Our server was a ladyboy with far too much make-up on. We ordered beers and were given an abrupt cold shoulder for turning the cocktails down.

"What's that about?" I mused.

Viktor shrugged. "I think they make a commission for selling watered-down cocktails?"

It made sense. Our beer arrived in glasses instead of the bottles we ordered and certainly tasted watered down. So we moved on. A few more bars with watered down beers until finally, we found a place called Jeje's offering a mix of bottled beers. A cute waitress there also promised really good non-watered down cocktails and so began our tasting session. She was right; they were good. Against the heat of the night, the fruity flavours went down well. As the drinks flowed, the music pumped louder, and we moved closer to the dance area. A couple of western girls were out on the floor so we joined in with their friends cheering us all on as two Thai girls joined us.

A hiss sounded, and a cloud of dry ice flowed onto the dance floor. The party was on as we all joined in dancing to the beats of a Lady GaGa remix without having a care in the world. It was no Haad Rin Beach and there was an element of darkness and seediness about Bangkok's nightspots, but I didn't care. I danced to enjoy myself. I danced to remember the good times, and I refused to let the bad memories come back. I danced, knowing I'd be going back to reality in a couple of days and life would not be the same again.

As the night moved on, Viktor broke out of his shell and had no problem building up the courage to dance with anyone. I'm not sure if it was the alcohol or exposure in southern Thailand or Julie's encouragement, but he was really getting into things on the dance floor. Finally, taking a breather, he joined me at the bar.

"Come on Jonny, these two girls are really into us, I can tell."

I looked out into the mass of people and shrugged. "Which two?"

Viktor turned and frowned. "No idea mate. They were there a second ago." He turned back to me and gave me one of his huge, sheepish grins. Only this time, I noticed something was off. His eyes were really big, like a semi startled rabbit.

"You okay, mate?"

"Yea, totally fine," he said, playing a drumbeat on the bar.

"You sure? You look a little wasted."

Viktor turned to me again, and I could clearly see he was not all there.

"Ya got me," he said, nearly falling off the barstool. "Ya got me."

"What?"

Viktor dug into his pocket and pulled out a little clear bag with three blue and white pills. "Got me some good-time fun before leaving the Pink Fish!"

"Shit man, put that away," I said, pushing his hand back. "Who'd you score that from?"

"Matt."

"Shit, how many did you take?"

"One," Viktor grinned. "Don't worry, mate, I'm not about to freak out or anything. I just want to have a good time. You want one?"

I was tempted. But truth be told, I didn't need anything to feel good. "No mate, it's cool. I'm doing great with the cocktails."

"Cool," nodded Viktor. "No worries. You want to try and find those two girls again?"

"Yea mate, no worries let's go find them."

We hit the dance floor and joined a throng of people. A mass of bodies all jumping and moving to the music. Another rush of dry ice gushed out, and we all cheered.

In the rush of heaving bodies, I met strangers, danced with them, and made trips back to the bar to rehydrate. I changed from cocktails to plain old red bull and then plain bottles of water. A guy at the bar asked why I wasn't drinking and all I could say was that I didn't need to. I was happy reaching a certain level and just wanted to enjoy the last of the parties.

***

By about two in the morning, I'd lost Viktor. There were people everywhere. I had no idea where he'd disappeared off to. The idea of him meeting a girl and sitting at a corner table somehow crossed my mind. I did a final walk around the outside of the dance floor, but I couldn't find him. All I got were random Thai girls coming up to me, wanting to know if I needed company. A brief thought crossed my mind about what would have happened if one of the girls had come up to Viktor in his current state and asked the same thing.

I sent him a message and noticed that he'd last been online about an hour ago and was now offline. Looking around outside offered no clues, either. The streets were empty apart from couples, a few scantily dressed people, and several prostitutes trying to pick up the nightclub leftovers. I asked the bouncer if he'd seen Viktor and then nodded at my own stupidity. The bouncer didn't speak English and didn't care about some English Indian guy who may or may not have left the building. I did one last tour of the dance floor area and went back to the guesthouse to see if he was there.

It cost me five hundred bhat in a taxi to go back. But at night

209

there was little traffic, and it was fast. I was honestly tired by this stage, so didn't care about the cost. What I did care about was that Viktor had the key to our room and that he was missing. I knocked on our door, but there was no answer. I went downstairs and asked if the receptionist had seen Viktor. The answer stunned me.

"Your frieeeend?" answered the male receptionist with a raised eyebrow. "Yes, he come back. In room now. You want another?"

"What? Really?"

"Yea, no problem," he said, scanning over his laptop booking sheet. "You wannnn room?"

"Why do I need another room?"

The receptionist looked at me with a blank expression.

"He got company."

I was stumped.

Lost for words, I thought about it for a while and then realised what the receptionist meant. I didn't have a place to sleep. My options were to ask for the spare key and interrupt Viktor. Or simply get my own room.

"Do you have a spare room?"

"two-thousand baht." replied the receptionist without hesitation.

"What, for a room?" I snapped. "I just need it for a few hours?"

"Two-thousand for private room like you have now."

"And a dorm bed?"

"Five hundred."

I took the dorm bed and surrendered to the thought of Viktor finally having a good story to tell tomorrow. Meanwhile, the dorm was full and very hot. It was a fan dorm. The air-conditioned room was fully occupied. I smiled to myself, knowing I shouldn't complain. Viktor did, after all, pay for our room. But at the same time, I couldn't help thinking I'd tease Viktor into buying me breakfast, lunch, and dinner for all this as I lay flat on a squeaky lower bunk. The fans' warm circulating air barely touched my skin. I sipped on a bottle of water and thought about the night with a smile.

By five, a series of snorers woke me. By six, two people turned on and off and on the lights before packing every rustling plastic bag they could into their backpacks. By seven, some older guy started smoking in the room, so I just quit the idea of sleep. Instead, I went to our room and listened at the door. There was silence. No noise, I was sure of it. I looked for a note or something from Viktor saying something like 'Jonny, I scored! Bugger off for the night, eh?' But there was nothing.

I chanced a knock on the door.

Silence.

There was no sound inside, I was sure of it. Not even a snore. And Viktor could snore. I knocked a little louder. Nothing. Well, if there was some hot passion going on, which I doubted, then they were being silent. Back downstairs and the receptionists were changing shifts.

"You think I could have the spare key to my room?" I asked, "I think my friend's just asleep now."

The night receptionist reached behind the desk and picked up a key. "Yes, your friend leave early today."

"Huh?"

"Good time night, then bye-bye," the two male receptionists laughed in a high pitch and giggled like schoolgirls.

I started to think they meant Viktor's girl had left early. I didn't care at this stage. I was tired and happy at the idea of catching up on some sleep before interrogating Viktor. Grabbing the key, I went back upstairs and quietly opened the door.

The curtains were closed, yet the strong Thai morning light still lit up the room. My bed was untouched. On the other side of the room, Viktor was under a bedsheet. Around his bed were the scatterings of some clothes and a general mess that told me he would wake up with an almighty hangover. And probably many good stories from the night before to keep him going for weeks, if not months, to come. I fell into bed and relaxed as a cool breeze from the air-conditioning unit fell over me. I heard Viktor move in his bed.

"Just me, mate, no worries," I said, pulling my sheet up and turning over. "Let me sleep for a few hours in peace, eh! Tell me about it later."

He grunted back.

I fell asleep quickly while thinking about Thai food, the dance floor, and Chinatown's mass of people. Then I moved on to Had Rin Beach. The bus trips. Smoking by a monastery. The mountains of Nepal. A flight to Bangkok. The dance floor again. A storm was approaching. A rainstorm. Heavy thunder clapped. Boom boom. Boom. BANG! Thai storms were so loud. BANG! BANG!

My eyes opened, and it took another few bangs before I realised where I was and what was happening. Someone was knocking loudly at the door. I looked over at Viktor's bed. He was gone. I cursed him and realised he must have locked himself out while getting breakfast or something.

Wrapped in a sheet, I shouted at the door to be quiet and slowly made my way over. Pulling the inner bolt open, my brain only just asked now how the inner bolt could be locked if Viktor had gone out. Then I heard a voice from outside that made my stomach lurch as I opened the door.

"Anne?"

"What the hell took you so long?"

I stood there and looked her up and down, blinking. It was Anne alright. Complete with all her bags and looking like she wanted to move in.

"What are you doing here?"

"What do you mean, what am I doing here? We're flying out tomorrow, aren't we?"

"Yea, but?"

"And how could you ever afford a double room like this?" she asked, pushing her bags through. "I inquired if you were in the dorm at reception and they just laughed."

My head throbbed, and I wondered why I even let her pass into the room. Outside, the receptionist was there staring at me as if waiting for permission to say everything was alright. I nodded at him and then waved goodbye as he shuffled off.

"Fucking no way?!"

"Huh," I turned back to Anne and saw her mouth drop. "What's wrong?"

Anne was just standing there, staring towards the bathroom. I moved around her and jumped back in shock.

"What you starrrring at?" said a high-pitched female voice.

Only the female voice didn't belong to a woman. There, standing in the doorway of the bathroom, was a topless ladyboy pulling a towel over her chest with one arm to cover up.

"Who the fuck are you?" I said, glaring as the skinny ladyboy sauntered over to the other bed.

"What you mean? I stay hhhhere."

"Fuck it Jonny," cursed Anne, breaking into a really nasty grin. "You're one twisted little man you know."

"What? She's not with me. I mean what the ..."

"I knew you were hard up, but this is pretty much answering a lot of questions about you, Jonny'

"Shut the fuck up Anne, this is nothing to do with me." I turned towards the ladyboy and tried to piece things together. "How did you get in here?"

The ladyboy pulled a bed sheet up around her entire body and then reached for a purse. "I stay here. I stay here with my very handsome man."

Fuck ... Viktor.

"I'm going to be sick," gaffed Anne.

"It's not me, Anne," I snarled before pointing at the ladyboy.

"Viktor? Where the hell is Viktor?"

"I don't know Viktor. I love my man."

Anne choked up again, "Shit Jonny, I never thought you'd go this way."

If ever I gave someone a look that said I was about to end them, Anne got it. She'd heard enough, though. Filled with her version of events, she pulled back towards the main door. But not without one last parting blow.

"I'll get my own room, Jonny," she smirked. "I don't want to interrupt your last night here."

The door clicked shut, and I turned to stare at the ladyboy as she opened a small makeup case and began powering her nose. What the hell had Viktor got up to last night?

The ladyboy was anything but helpful in answering my questions. My head was spinning, and I really couldn't work out where Viktor was, either. It was only when I looked inside the bathroom I noticed his wash bag was gone. Then inside the room, I noticed his bag was also gone. The only thing of his left were a couple of odd socks and a t-shirt on the ground.

Back at the reception desk, things fell into place when I asked straightforward questions. It wasn't a lady that left early that morning. It was Viktor. Knowing you sometimes have to answer your own questions in Thailand to get an answer, I asked if he'd left a note. The receptionist handed me a folded up piece of paper.

Jonny mate,
Sorry about last night. It got a little wild and crazy. I broke the screen on my phone too.
I've paid for the room and left the receipt in the corner pocket of your backpack. I also left you some money between your guidebook photocopy pages. Pages two-hundred to two-hundred thirty. They're where you always hide your backup cash. Should cover you for a few last meals here.
Good luck, mate. And thanks for a blast.
See you in Blighty some time. You have my number.
Vik

***

The flight back home was a little surreal. Anne never said a word. She sat by the window seat, reading a book about reincarnation for the first few hours. Even when she got up to use the bathroom, she said nothing. She just stood up and nodded towards the aisle.

It was on my own bathroom break that I asked the flight attendant if I could move seats. There were a few available towards the rear and if anything, I wanted the extra space. The flight attendant wasn't too keen. She had a French accent, seemed stern, and was none too happy about me breaking up her routine. So I gave an honest reason.

"We broke up on our holiday." I nodded my head towards Anne and my empty seat beside her.

"Oh!" the flight attendant's stern face looked instantly sad. "I'm so sorry."

"It's no problem," I smiled back gently. "I could just do with some alone time. If you know what I mean?"

The flight attendant broke into a sympathetic smile as if she had all the inside knowledge in the world.

"But of course," she said in reassuring confidence. "Take that seat there."

It must be a universal thing. Breaking up and the feelings thereafter. Everyone's been there and knows what it's like. I was well over it, but I'd be damned if Anne was going to make the last leg of my trip a miserable one.

The flight attendant brought me some extra snacks, a Wi-Fi voucher, and a look as if she wanted to ask me all about it, but couldn't. Well, working at thirty-five-thousand feet does have its limitations when it comes to having a shoulder to cry on. Not that I wanted to. But I was grateful that the attendant cared enough in this day and age.

All in all, I was feeling quite good. A little shell-shocked from the events of the last 24 hours. But I think that's understandable, all things considered.

I looked at the movie list on the seat's touch screen in front of me. Flicking through them, I began to settle on what to watch to pass the time. Nothing jumped out. Nothing really compared to life over the past few months. It seemed like such a waste to just pass the time away on the last part of this journey. Maybe I'd already done enough of that over the past few years. I remembered the Wi-Fi voucher. I typed it into my phone.

I paused.

When the plane landed, life would be back to normal again. Instead of hanging on or passing time, I typed.

Jobs for a year.

Jobs after travelling.

I caught a glimpse of the flight attendant. I typed again.

Jobs in … France?

CHAPTER 25

BACK IN LONDON

Being back in London for over a month wasn't as traumatic as I thought it would have been. I didn't get the whole reverse culture shock thing I'd read about since coming back. I was simply happy to be back. I could eat food that wasn't made from unidentifiable animal parts, and my clothes were actually clean after a wash. I didn't sweat as soon as I came out of the shower. Even my dental check-up didn't involve drugs, drink, or vast quantities of panic.

In fairness to the Nepali dentist, my family dentist said he'd done a good job. And, after my mother insisted I go to a tropical disease clinic for a full battery of tests, I got the all-clear. I was going to go anyway, but it also put her mind at ease.

What had changed was that I didn't find things traumatic any more. I'd see a homeless person on the street and instead of looking away, I'd stare into their eyes. I remember this from Nepal. The lost look. Or the hungry look that never leaves you once you've seen the worst of it. Then, just like on the streets of Kathmandu, I'd often give them the other half of my sandwich rather than money. In Kathmandu, they'd often sell sealed food items back to the shops for money to buy drugs or booze. I figured they'd do the same here, too.

The fun and adventure of Thailand was certainly lacking in London. For a capital city, it lacked the freedom of just about anywhere in Thailand. I noticed that I now had to watch what I said as everyone back home seemed to take offense to 'everything' these days. In short, the reality of it all was that I actually missed all the craziness of the trip. Everything back home was just so ordinary and restraining.

However, what had been continually traumatising me were messages from Charles wanting to meet up since I came back. And that's where I was now. At our old local pub, sitting and waiting for him to show up. I'd not spoken to Anne since she left my room in Bangkok. We'd remained silent on the plane and at the airport. We simply separated at Heathrow and made our own way back to our respective homes. I'd no idea what she told Charles. This would have worried me once. Now it just irritated me.

"Jonny!"

It was Charles from across the beer garden. He waved at me and made a drinking gesture with his hand. I held up a half pint and nodded. It seemed all was well with him. So he must not have been told any 'stories.'

Then, like a ghostly widow, Anne appeared from behind him. She looked awkward and clearly didn't want to be there. Charles pointed to me with a smile and urged her forward while moving to the bar to get the drinks. Anne glared in my direction and I could see her jaw twitch even from this distance. Reluctantly, she came over and my eyes fixated on her to see if there would be any communication at all. She gave me a sour glare. I remained calm.

She sat down and said nothing.

I could have let it all slip away, but I had no idea what she'd told Charles about our trip. Good or bad, I think it was right to at least clear the air. If not, then so be it.

"How much does he know?"

Anne's jaw clenched. She stayed silent for longer than normal. Glancing over at Charles as he picked up a tray at the bar, she turned to me. "He knows you're a jerk."

"Oh, piss off Anne."

"Fuck you."

"Hey guys," Charles put the tray down and placed a pint in front of me. Then extended a hand. "Good to see you again Jonny."

I looked at my old school chum and shook his hand back, "You to Charles, always."

"Yea, we should have met up when you guys got back, but I've been so caught up in this legal bar thing it's taken all my time."

"How's it going?"

"It's over, for now," he said, rubbing his unshaven face. He'd put on a bit of weight since the last time we'd met. "Who'd ever want to work in the field of law after all this crap."

Then there was an awkward lull in the conversation. Two old friends and a sister of one that the other had slept with, that the other didn't know about who then fell apart on holiday in a bout of mutual hatred. What was there to say in a situation like this?

"So you two have been really quiet about your grand adventure in the east." Charles finally chimed in.

Anne raised her eyebrows and forced a grin.

I turned my lips inside out and then took a drink, wondering who would say what first. Instead, we all fell back into another awkward silence. This was possibly the worst thing to do around a man who wanted to be a barrister. He wanted answers, not silence.

"So I guess you guys had a big fight or something, huh?"

I snorted a refrained laugh, "Let's just say we won't be doing something like that again in a hurry."

"That bad, eh?"

Anne took a sip from her glass of vodka. "Some people just aren't cut out for travel."

"Yea," laughed Charles unknowingly. "I could never really imagine you up in the mountains somehow, Jonny."

"I'm actually going back to Nepal next year," I confessed.

"What?" sneered Anne. "You hated the place?"

"Yea, I did," I confessed again. "But I think it was the situation I hated more than the place."

Anne glared at me, "Yea, some people just can't handle certain situations."

I looked over at Charles. He also knew when it was better to say nothing if he wanted answers.

Silence.

Fuck it.

I wasn't going to let it slide.

Here we go.

"Yea mate, shit like that happens when you get ditched and then left behind after breaking a tooth abroad."

"I didn't ditch you," interrupted Anne. "Everything was already arranged for the trek."

"So you know," I continued. "I never got a chance to actually go trekking."

"Ha!" interrupted Anne, again. "You didn't want to go, anyway."

I ignored her and continued on, "So I sent Stuart, this trekking writer guy we met, an email through his website when I got back."

Anne's eyes suddenly widened.

I had been saving this up for so long.

"He's actually the guy who took Anne trekking. And I asked him about doing the Everest Base Camp trek next year. Nice guy, sent me a load of information."

"You couldn't stand Stuart," snapped Anne.

"He's okay, actually." I was about to chance a half-truth. "Told me a lot about what the monks get up to over there too."

"Don't start," said Anne, forcibly biting her lower lip.

I waited for a few microseconds to pass. "What? Like sleeping with volunteers?"

"FUCK YOU!" spat Anne. The gloves were off and her jaw went into hyper pulsating mode. "How dare you say something like that?"

"Yea Jonny," frowned Charles suddenly looking confused by how quickly everything had collapsed. "Steady on mate."

"See?" Anne held her hand out at me while staring at her brother.

"This is the type of prick your mate Jonny really is. This is the type of jealous bullshit I've had to put up with this whole time. Just because I wouldn't sleep with him."

"What?" I gasped. "Fuck you, Anne. We did sleep together. Plenty of times. Before we left. Long before we left. And in Thailand! Before you went off with a monk who most likely stole my laptop too!"

Charles was not looking happy. But surprisingly, said nothing. Anne was the one making up for that.

"Bollox. You're a little shit Jonny, who did everything he could to get me into bed and couldn't get the job done when he did."

By now we'd attracted the curious ears of the neighbouring tables in the beer garden. Even as far back as the bar. Anne was staring between Charles and me while twisting her glass on the table.

I stared at her accusingly while fleeting looks at Charles as well. Instead of anger or self-defence, though, I felt something else. A sadness. I saw something happening that was forcing two old schoolmates who grew up together to choose the inevitable. And fall apart.

"I'm sorry, Charles," I said, shaking my head in confession. "The truth is, we did spend time together. We broke up before leaving. The trip was a nightmare."

"Bollox," interrupted Anne. "That's horseshit. It was a bad one-night stand that dragged on for too long."

"We went on holiday," I continued. "Went to a beach place. I got caught smoking a spliff. Anne threw a fit."

"Stop it, Jonny."

"We flew to Nepal. I broke my tooth. Anne fucked off trekking with this guy Stuart and a Monk. Came back and the monk stole my laptop."

"What?" shrieked Anne. "See what I mean Charles? Off he goes with his horseshit again. A monk stole his laptop?"

"Yea," I said, tapping my pint glass. "This is the same monk you were holding hands with at the monastery."

"Fuck you!" Anne threw her vodka over my chest and stood up. "At least I didn't shag a ladyboy in Bangkok!"

Well, if there was a last straw. Anne had just dropped it. Something that, understandably, had the whole pub staring at our table.

Charles stood up and looked at his sister, who was feigning tears. Then he looked at me. His eyes showed the choice he had to make. Putting his arm on Anne's elbow, they turned and left.

I sat there and mopped up the vodka on my shirt. The bar had had their evening's worth of entertainment. I could hear the whispers mentioning 'ladyboy' more times than I was comfortable with. What could I do? I sat there and pulled out my phone with one hand while finishing my pint with the other.

Flicking down to messages, I pulled up the last received message.

Parents just leased me an apartment in London. Wanna come to my moving in party mate? It won't be like Thailand, but anyway :)

I hit reply.

I wouldn't miss it, Viktor. See you next Saturday.

Leaving the pub in a haze of gossip, I wondered if life always changed so dramatically whenever you went travelling? Maybe it's the places or the people. Life seemed so monotonous back home. I now had my goal for next year. I'd been accepted by a French holiday apparel shop catering to English-speaking tourists for a summer job. I'd be sharing a house with two others from Europe. I calculated that by the end of the summer, I'd have saved quite a bit.

For the first time in my life, I had a goal to achieve by myself. And some penance to pay to the mountains I never climbed but was now eager to conquer.

It seemed I was beginning to like travel after all.

A NOTE FROM THE AUTHOR

First, let me take this opportunity to thank you for purchasing this book, and reading it. I'm figuring you read it all the way through to get here! There are no spoilers if you are just flicking through the book at a store right now. (Yes, it's good, buy it.)

I wrote this book, at a time when I needed to laugh.

It worked. Well, it worked for me. Even after many, many edits I still crack a smile at Jonny's exploits as he finds his way through life and the world, on his journey. My hope is that you also laughed at Jonny's antics, mishaps and misadventures. If so, mission accomplished.

If you have the time, leave a review of this book with your thoughts on it. Amazon, Goodreads, etc,.

(Warning, incoming sales pitch) To be one step ahead of Jonny, and if you ever think of venturing to the top of the world yourself do check out my guidebooks. Yes, they are far, far more serious in tone and are actually factual. However, they'll also make your trip to Nepal so much better because ...

Nobody Should Forget Their Guidebook!

Meanwhile, I'm human! Feel free to say hello.

www.thelongestwayhome.com

ABOUT THE AUTHOR

David Ways began an epic journey in 2005 to travel the world in search of a home. He travelled solo overland from Sintra in Portugal across Europe into Iran, Pakistan, India and Nepal where he discovered the feeling called home. After that, he travelled up into Tibet overland into China to the far east before exploring the rest of South-East Asia.

Throughout his life, David documented his journeys using everything from notepads to email drafts to writing on one of the very first blogging platforms to creating www.thelongestwayhome. com. It was on this website that David began writing out practical, frank and detailed travel guides to help fill the gap that commercial travel guidebooks left out. There was no looking back.

For over 14 years David has created what is today the worlds number one online travel guide to Nepal (he's working on a few other countries as well). He's created and continues to publish innovative live interactive digital guidebooks to Nepal which have changed the way many people travel the country.

In 2015 David founded the Digital Archaeology Foundation to help preserve Nepal's cultural heritage digitally for future generations.

In 2016 David launched MissingTrekker.com. A website portal to help the family and friends of trekkers who go missing in Nepal.

In 2017 his Nepal guidebook was published in paperback by Himalayan Travel Guides and became a national bestseller.

Throughout all these years David's been taking notes, logging and documenting Nepali heritage for another project. In 2018 he spent the year piecing everything together for what would become the Kathmandu Valley's largest, most thorough and most concise book on Kathmandu Valley Heritage Walks.

In 2019 Kathmandu Valley Heritage Walks was published in paperback along with the second paperback edition of the Nepal Guidebook.

Despite the 2019 pandemic, David continued to update his guidebooks both online and in print.

In 2020 David released a coffee table photograph book entitled Kathmandu: Signs of the Past.

In 2021 special second edition print versions of the Nepal Guidebook and Kathmandu Valley Heritage Walks were published.

In 2022 David published a new Hiking and Trekking Journal logbook along with this book: Don't Forget Your Guidebook.

MORE BOOKS BY THE AUTHOR

<u>SCAN THE CODE ABOVE TO CHECK OUT
MY FULL GUIDEBOOKS TO NEPAL & OTHER
GREAT BOOKS</u>

www.thelongestwayhome.com